# READ ALL THE SPY KIDS™ ADVENTURES!

## COMING SOON!

# SPY KIDS™
## ADVENTURES
### SPY TV

Based on the characters
by Robert Rodriguez

Written by Elizabeth Lenhard

VOLO

HYPERION
MIRAMAX BOOKS
New York

Printed in the United States of America

First Edition

1 3 5 7 9 10 8 6 4 2

This book is set in 13/17 New Baskerville.

ISBN 0-7868-1804-2

Visit www.spykids.com

# CHAPTER 1

It was a ho-hum morning in the Cortez family's sunny kitchen. Mom was practicing her roundhouse kicks on the breakfast-nook punching bag. Dad was sipping *café con leche* and reading a top secret brief from the president. And their twelve-year-old daughter, Carmen, was testing a new gadget called the Insta-UnderCover Cap. It had just arrived in the mail from her inventor uncle.

The moment Carmen placed the green woolly hat on her head, her dark, wavy locks went straight and blond. Her almond-shaped eyes morphed from brown to blue and the freckles on her nose melted away. Carmen glanced at her reflection in the Cortezes' robotic toaster and gasped. She was virtually unrecognizable!

And this was a good thing. Because Carmen Cortez was a spy. So was her younger brother, Juni. And so were their parents. In fact, all four of the Cortezes worked for a secret government agency called the Office of Strategic Services.

At the OSS, Carmen and Juni were stars of the Spy Kids division. They had an ever-expanding arsenal of spy gadgets. They were kung fu masters who spoke more than a dozen languages. Carmen was a brilliant computer hacker. Juni was a gourmet chef.

Since one should never send an adult to do a kid's job, Carmen and Juni were regularly sent around the globe to save the world.

But that didn't mean they weren't also ordinary kids. Take Juni, for instance. While his sister was shape-shifting over by the toaster, he was sitting next to his dad at the table, devouring a giant bowl of marshmallowy cereal and staring at the TV on the kitchen counter. A booming voice rang from the tube.

"It's that time of day," an announcer trilled. "Time for you to *Rise & Shine with Cayenne Coyer!*"

Juni shoved another big spoonful of cereal into his mouth as the *Cayenne Coyer* studio audience roared with approval. Then a skinny woman with a helmet of glistening blond hair and loads of mascara walked onto the set, which was decorated with couches, coffee tables, and other homey types of furniture.

"Have we got a show for you today!" Cayenne

chirped, clapping her manicured hands together with delight. "We'll be talking to that pro wrestler we all love—Goldstein!"

More whoops and applause from the audience.

"We'll also tell you five *unexpected* ways to rid your T-shirts of unsightly armpit stains," Cayenne burbled. "But first, let's meet a very lucky family of four. They've just been chosen to compete on *Power Trip!*"

As a couple of well-groomed kids and their parents trooped onto the stage, Juni sighed with longing. A few cereal crumbs blew out of his mouth.

"*Power Trip!*" he said to Carmen, who was still across the kitchen checking out her new look. "That's supposed to be, like, the hottest new reality show ever! Really brutal!"

"*Power Trip,*" Cayenne twittered, "which will air in a few months on our very own MYPQ network, promises to be, like, the hottest new reality show ever."

"See!" Juni said with a nod.

Carmen rolled her eyes.

"I'm *so-o-o* impressed," she growled. Then she clapped a hand over her mouth. Her voice was several octaves lower than usual! And it was as gravelly as a dirt road.

"What's with your voice?" Juni said. "Talk about a frog in your throat!"

Carmen snatched the Insta-UnderCover Cap from her head. As her hair and eyes darkened once again, she uttered a tentative, "Testing, one, two, three!" Then she sighed with relief. Her voice had returned to normal.

"I'll have to get Uncle Machete to iron out this cap's kinks," she said, shaking her head. Their dad's brother, Machete, was a superbrilliant spy gadget inventor. Unfortunately, his gizmos—like the Insta-UnderCover Cap—often arrived with a few glitches.

"Shhh!" Juni said, turning back to the TV. "I want to see who's going to be on *Power Trip*!"

Carmen sat down at the table and poured herself her own bowl of cereal. On TV, Cayenne Coyer invited the family to sit on a couch.

"Well, America," she announced, "meet the Cheathams! Rich, Margarita, and their adorable kids, Allie and Tate!"

The audience showered the guests with more whoops, whistles, and foot stomps.

"So tell us, Rich," Cayenne said, turning to the dad. "How does it feel to be the very first contestants on *Power Trip*?"

Rich ran a hand over his hair, which was as blond and perfectly shellacked as Cayenne's. Then he smiled and said, "Well, we're just thrilled to bits. I mean, sure, the wife and kids and I are living a life anybody would envy. After inheriting my fortune from my great-grandfather, we invested wisely and began living the good life. We winter in the South of France and summer at our vineyard in northern California. We spring on our Vermont dairy farm and autumn in New York. The kids are doing smashingly at their East Coast boarding schools, and our marriage is blissful. Still, one day, I looked at my lovely wife and said, 'Darling, where's the *challenge*?'"

"Ees trrrrue," Margarita said in a thick, rich Argentinean accent, rolling Rs and all.

"I told Daddy I was all for *Power Trip*," piped up the teenage daughter, Allie. She pooched out her glossy lips and gazed earnestly into the camera. "*If* we could donate our prize money to charity, of course!"

"But *I* get to keep the Armadillo Wax," cried Tate, who looked like he was about eight. He had mischievous dark eyes and his mother's glossy black hair.

The studio audience roared with laughter while Cayenne clasped her hands in admiration.

"Well, aren't you a special bunch!" she cooed. "But are you sure you're ready for the rigors of *Power Trip*? After all, contestants will be stranded for an entire week on a remote island. It's been stocked with all sorts of pitfalls, from critters to crevasses. I hear the TV crew can be pretty crabby, too!"

Cayenne winked at the audience.

"Oh, we're rrrrrready," Margarita declared, tossing a black ringlet over her tanned shoulder. "I just hope the other contestants are worthy foes!"

"Frankly, I think you Cheathams will be a tough act to follow!" Cayenne warbled. Then she turned to the camera. "And what family is going to step up to the plate? Tune in tomorrow. We'll be announcing the challengers right here on *Rise & Shine with Cayenne Coyer*!"

As the studio audience whistled and shouted, Juni turned down the TV's volume.

"Ooooh," he sighed longingly. "That show is *so* made for us. We'd kick the Cheathams' butts!"

"Yeah, but we'd have to do it on TV!" Carmen cried. "Ew!"

"Ew?!" Juni yelled. "Ew?! Carmen, are you crazy? Do you know what happens to people who go on reality TV shows? They become *famous*. They get invited to all the coolest parties! They ride limos wherever they go. They have fans. They get to go on talk shows and exchange jokes with guys like Keenan O'Ryan. They get a lifetime supply of . . . Armadillo Wax!"

"What is Armadillo Wax?" Carmen wondered aloud, crunching her cereal.

"I don't know, but they're *always* talking about it on TV," Juni said reverentially. "So it's gotta be good."

Carmen rolled her eyes and reached over to the counter to click the television off.

"You're brainwashed," Carmen said. "Living on camera for an entire week would be completely humiliating. Not to mention a major job hazard."

Mom, who'd just finished her workout and sat slumped sweatily in a kitchen chair, nodded in agreement.

"Sorry, fella, but your sister's right," she said. "Spies are supposed to fly under the radar. Fame is definitely not our M.O."

Now Dad looked up from his report.

"And besides," he protested, "I could never let your mother go on TV. She's so pretty, she'd be besieged by fan mail. And you know how I tend to get pretty jealous!"

"Oh, Gregorio!" Mom said, wiping her neck with a towel.

"Oh, Ingrid," Dad said, smiling.

"Oh, man," Carmen protested. "Please don't get mushy on us. We're eating breakfast here!"

While Mom and Dad giggled, Juni slumped back in his chair.

". . . wanna be on TV," he muttered, ". . . *Power Trip* . . . fame . . . fortune . . . no fair . . ."

The boy spy was working himself into a real sulk-fest. But before he could get *really* upset, a noise filled the Cortezes' mansion. Juni's ears perked up and his scowl turned into a broad grin.

"Whoo-hoo," he cried. "That's a sound almost as sweet as an announcer saying, 'And now, back to our program!' It's the OSS alarm! Mission time!"

The moment the sirens quit blaring, the blank television screen sprang back to life. Filling the screen was the broad-shouldered torso of the Cortezes' boss, Diego Devlin.

Angling his strong-jawed face this way and that, he said to someone behind the TV camera, "I can never remember—which is my good side? Right or left?"

"Left, sir. Definitely left," said a muffled voice.

Devlin flashed a thumbs-up and turned his face to the right. He patted his head to make sure no hairs were loose, fixed his shirt, and checked his breath. Then he gave his spies a wave and his trademark rakish grin.

"Cortezes," he announced. "It's mission time. Get ready for your close-up!"

# CHAPTER 2

**A**s the spies stared seriously at the television, Devlin began to explain their mission.

"Your foes are a family of four by the name of Cheatham," he said.

"The Cheathams?!" Juni squeaked. "But I just saw them on TV."

"Therein lies the problem," Devlin said. "The OSS has been tracking this family for a while. Their spokesman is the father, Rich. He's cool as a cucumber and slick as a slug. But the real brains behind the operation is Allie."

"The daughter?" Carmen said, raising one of her eyebrows.

"On the surface, she's an ordinary fourteen-year-old," Devlin said. As he spoke, his face faded and a photo of Allie filled the screen. She was tall and lissome, with honey-colored hair cascading around her shoulders. Her chocolate brown eyes were glittery and knowing. Her cheekbones were high, and her clothes were stylin'. In short, she was fabulously cool.

"Underneath that glossy smile," Devlin continued, "is an evil mastermind at work. At her father's request, Allie has devised this!"

Devlin reappeared on the television and held up a glittery blue bracelet. The spies looked at one another and shrugged. Then Mom cleared her throat and asked diplomatically, "So is this a case of, uh, copyright infringement? Jewelry cartel? Perhaps a violation of antitackiness laws?"

"No, Ingrid," Devlin said. "This is a re-creation of Allie Cheatham's Brain Beater. It looks like an ordinary bracelet. But in actuality, it's a powerful hormone atomizer. One zap with this baby and Allie can manipulate you to do anything she wants—from robbing a bank to giving her her own TV show."

Juni gasped in horror. "Evil!" he said.

"Oh, it gets worse, kiddo," Devlin replied. "You see, Allie's little bauble here works best when diffused over television airwaves."

"You don't mean . . . ?"

"I do," Devlin replied. "The Cheathams have insinuated themselves into the spotlight for one purpose. They want to use their on-camera time to hypnotize the TV-viewing public. With enough TV exposure, the Cheathams could collect millions of minions."

Juni placed his trembling hands on top of the television set. He thrust his pale face up close to the screen. His beloved TV—an instrument of evil? How could it be?!

Suddenly, Juni jumped backward.

"Uh, thanks, Juni," Devlin said with a curled lip. "You were fogging up the screen there."

"I just realized something," Juni announced. "The Cheathams can't hypnotize the masses from *Power Trip*. The show's gonna be taped and won't be broadcast for months. Wouldn't they need a live feed?"

"Yes, they would," Devlin said.

"Ha-ha!" Juni cried triumphantly.

"And they'll get plenty of live TV time if they win *Power Trip*," Devlin continued. "With all those late-night talk shows, on-camera celebrity parties, and movie premieres, they'll saturate the media in no time. I've already heard a show biz rumor—if the Cheathams win, Cayenne Coyer wants to give them their own cooking segment on her morning show."

Suddenly, Juni drifted off into a daydream. He saw himself in front of a studio audience, a tall, white chef's hat planted on top of his unruly red curls. He was suavely sautéing vegetables in a copper skillet. Blazing down upon him was the sunny smile of Cayenne Coyer.

"Chef Juni Cortez," she cooed, "please, tell us about this morning's masterpiece!"

Juni didn't look up from his pan as he replied, in a silky French accent, "Eez a seemple, but oh-so-elegant, crepe with truffles, lobster, haricots verts, and, of course, zee pièce de résistance . . . an entire kilo of clarified butter."

The studio audience gasped in awe.

"Oh, Chef Cortez," Cayenne burbled. "It's a meal fit for a king."

"Well," Juni said with a humble shrug, "zee president of zee United States seemed to enjoy it when I served it at zee White House last week. . . ."

Juni was jolted out of his reverie by the thunk of Carmen's knuckles on his head.

"Earth to spy boy," she whispered. "We're in the middle of a briefing and you're drooling through a daydream!"

Shaking off his sister, Juni refocused on Devlin. Then he announced in a determined voice, "Mr. Devlin! We *can't* let the Cheathams win *Power Trip*!"

"My thoughts exactly," Devlin said, nodding in approval. "Instead, *you're* going to."

Carmen gasped. Suddenly, *she* drifted off into a daydream. She was crouched on a beach like a feral child, being interviewed by the host of a reality TV show.

"So, Carmen," the host was saying, his voice dripping with faux gentleness. "Tell us what went wrong out there today."

"Hey, *you* try to eat a handful of centipedes and *then* we'll talk," Carmen replied sullenly. She ran a hand over her head in a futile effort to smooth her sand-caked hair.

"I'm sure things will go better at the tapeworm rodeo tomorrow," the host chirped encouragingly.

"Tapeworms?!" Carmen shrieked.

Suddenly, she turned to the host and grabbed his shirt collar.

"Listen, you," she sputtered. "I can hack into any computer in the world. I know kung fu, jujitsu, and shiatsu massage. I speak Cantonese *and* Mandarin, and I can even sing. I have just *one* hang-up. One! And that's bugs!"

"Ooh, too bad," the host said. "I hear we're having salt-and-pepper grubs for dinner tonight."

"Aaaaaaiiiigh!" Carmen screamed in horror.

"Oh, and Carmen?" the host said, in closing. "I hate to tell you this after you've just *finished* an interview that will be viewed by millions of TV viewers, but you've got a gnarly centipede leg stuck between your teeth. . . ."

Carmen was jolted from her horrible fantasy by her brother's elbow jabbing her in the ribs.

"Who's drooling through a mission briefing now?" he whispered gleefully. Carmen shook her head blearily. Luckily, Devlin hadn't noticed her lack of focus. In fact, he was giving the spies a good-bye salute. Then the TV screen went black.

As soon as Devlin disappeared, Juni started jumping up and down in excitement.

"Whoo-hoo!" he cried. "This is the coolest mission ever! We're gonna be on TV!"

"Oh. My. God," Carmen moaned, laying her head on the kitchen table. "The humiliation."

Dad, meanwhile, was gazing into his reflection in the toaster and sucking in his gut.

"Ingrid," he said with a slight tremor in his voice. "That isn't really true, is it? That the camera adds ten pounds?"

"Not now, honey," Mom replied distractedly. She was heading out of the kitchen. "I have to go upstairs and start packing. This trip's going to call for lots of lipstick and plenty of under-eye concealer."

"Not to mention our coolest gadgets!" Juni

cried. While his family quietly freaked out about becoming famous, he bounded over to the kitchen's emergency gear vault. (It was cleverly disguised as a trash compactor.) He pulled out a bag labeled "Desert Island Gizmos." He was just tossing the bag into a larger backpack when, suddenly, another siren went off.

But this wasn't the OSS mission alert. This alarm was more shrill, more urgent, and, most of all, louder.

The Cortez mansion's security had been breached!

The four spies were dispersed around the kitchen. They had only seconds to shoot one another surprised glances before the room filled with ten big, burly men in military fatigues.

The lead soldier grinned at the spies through his camouflage face paint.

"Ready for prime time?" he asked them.

"What do you mean?" Dad sputtered as he dropped into a martial-arts fighting stance.

The soldiers didn't answer. They were too busy ambushing the entire family! Even for the Cortezes, ten commandos were a lot to kibosh, so it didn't take long for the soldiers to overpower the family completely. In minutes, the spies were cuffed and yanked out of their cozy kitchen.

As the soldiers led the family to a small cargo plane parked on their expansive lawn, Juni shot Carmen a megadisappointed look.

"Of all the times to be taken hostage," he complained. "Just when I was closing in on my fifteen minutes of fame!"

# CHAPTER 3

**C**armen sat strapped into a helicopter seat. She was blindfolded and gagged. And, boy, was she mad!

Our mission hasn't even begun yet, she thought indignantly, and we've already been kidnapped?! Are we losing our touch or what?

Of course, she'd barely finished her silent sulk when she felt her mother's elbow touch hers. And on her other side, Juni was nudging her with his shoulder. She could tell—they were ready to take action!

Carmen nudged them back to let them know she was listening. Then Mom tapped her elbow six times—two short taps and two long ones, followed by one short and one long.

Carmen caught her breath. Her mom was speaking to her in code! And Carmen got the signal loud and clear: in exactly two minutes, the four spies would execute one of their most theatrical kick-butt maneuvers—the Barnum & Bailey.

Carmen sent Juni the same taps.

Then she braced herself for action and counted down the seconds. As she counted, she knew her dad was using the laser he'd recently had installed in one of his front teeth to burn away his gag. Then he'd scorch his way through the ropes around his wrists and untie his blindfold.

When her countdown reached zero, Carmen thrust her bound hands out in front of her. She felt a little sizzle as the laser beam sliced through the ropes around her wrists. Dad moved on to Juni and Mom while Carmen untied her blindfold and snapped open her seat belt. In seconds, her entire family was free. They looked around. Sitting all around them were their kidnapping commandos! The soldiers were unbuckling their seat belts and growling at the spies. Juni responded by dropping to his knees and throwing out his arms.

"Hey, guys," he yelled. "Welcome to the greatest show on earth!"

With that, Dad cupped his hands close to the floor. Carmen stepped into them and Dad tossed her up toward the plane's ceiling. She grabbed a bar and began swinging back and forth in long, graceful arcs.

Juni grabbed his sister's ankles and started swinging with her. Every time a commando lunged at him, Juni took the soldier down with a superfast karate kick.

*Thwack, thwack, thwack!*

Juni had downed three soldiers in three seconds. Now it was time for his big finish! He let go of Carmen's ankles, did a somersault in midair, then landed in the center of the plane with his fists raised.

"Anybody else?" he asked threateningly.

The soldiers shook their heads in awe and backed away slowly.

Now it was Mom and Dad's turn to kick it into gear. Mom climbed onto Dad's shoulders. Then she paused for a moment, looking for the best target. Should she go for the soldier cowering by the galley? Or the small guy fiddling with his helmet?

"Oh, what the heck," Mom muttered with a shrug. "I'll take 'em both."

She raised her arms over her head and got ready to pounce. But at the last moment, she was distracted by the short soldier. He'd unclasped his chin strap and whipped the helmet off his head.

Make that *her* head. *He* was a *she*!

And talk about hat hair! Beneath the soldier's hard hat was *another* helmet. This one was made of glistening blond, practically painted-on hair. Hair that could only belong to . . .

"This is Cayenne Coyer!" the woman announced. She pulled a microphone from her camouflage jacket. Then she turned to a fellow soldier, who whipped a TV camera out of *his* jacket. "I'm reporting to you for MYPQ—live!"

"Live?!" Juni said, his eyes lighting up.

"Live?" Carmen squeaked, falling to the plane floor with a thud.

"Live . . ." Mom said in a stunned rasp. She jumped off her husband's shoulders and smoothed down her disheveled ginger-colored hair. Then she sidled over to her family and whispered, "You think our cover is blown?"

"Not if we pretend to be a family of circus freaks!" Carmen hissed back. Then she dropped her face into her hands. This was *so* humiliating.

For *some* of them, anyway . . .

"Cayenne!" Juni cried. He bounded across the cargo plane and placed himself squarely in the TV camera's spotlight. "What a nice surprise to see you here . . . as we're being . . . uh, kidnapped?"

"Oh, no, Juni Cortez!" Cayenne burbled. She patted Juni's head. "These are not actually paramilitary commandos at all. They're TV producers, directors, and writers. And *you're* the new contestants on . . . *Power Trip*!"

"This kidnapping was all a ruse?" Dad cried, bounding up behind his son. "Of all the crass, irresponsible, ridiculous, publicity-mongering . . ."

Before Dad could add any more adjectives to his rant, Mom ran over to the camera, too. She clapped a hand over Dad's mouth, then grinned at the camera extra hard.

"My husband!" she giggled. "*Such* a kidder! Of course, we're thrilled to be the next contestants on *Power Trip*."

Dad's eyes widened.

"Oh . . . oh, yes, of course," he said, extricating himself from Mom's grip and sucking in his gut quickly. "What I meant to say was . . . *clever* ruse. Very clever!"

"Why, thank you!" Cayenne cooed. Then she motioned to a tarp-covered pile at one end of the cargo plane. One of the fake soldiers ripped the tarp away to reveal a red couch, a couple of chairs, and a coffee table stocked with *Rise & Shine* mugs. Juni rushed to grab the seat closest to Cayenne.

The rest of the family sat down next to him. They regarded the TV camera edgily and tried to smooth their kidnapping-mussed outfits.

"So, let's learn a few things about our new *Power Trip* family," Cayenne cooed. "Gregorio, Ingrid, Carmen, and Juni Cortez. What interesting names."

"Well, yes, I am Spanish, you know," Dad said proudly.

"Uh-huh!" Cayenne said. "And do *you* have a second home in Europe like the Cheathams?"

"Uh, no . . ." Dad said with a befuddled frown. "We have just one home. But it's a very nice one. On a cliff!"

"Uh-huh," Cayenne said, sounding bored. "Now, as you undoubtedly know, Rich Cheatham is an heir to a fortune, a winemaker, the chairman of the board of his family foundation, etc., etc. And what do *you* do?"

"Well . . ." Dad said, shooting his family a nervous glance.

"Uh, we're computer consultants, Cayenne," Mom said.

Cayenne's face fell. So did Juni's. Computer consulting was so . . . glamourless!

And the irony is, Juni thought indignantly, it's not even true! Not anymore.

Once upon a time, Mom and Dad *had* been consultants. They'd taken on the job after they'd dropped out of the dangerous spy game. (*That* had happened when they'd become parents. They'd decided they wanted a life that was safe; a life without secrets.)

But when Juni was eight, his parents had been lured into one last spy mission. They couldn't resist the opportunity to save the world. Unfortunately, they'd botched the mission badly—they had been a little out of practice. So, Carmen and Juni had come to their rescue. That was when the entire family had become spies.

But every spy needs a cover—a false identity he or she can present to the world. And the Cortezes' cover was "computer consultants."

*We* should have said we were winemakers or heirs to a family fortune, Juni thought with a sigh. Then maybe Cayenne Coyer wouldn't be looking at us like we're gum on her expensive Italian shoes. Hmm, maybe this TV thing is going to be more challenging than I thought.

Cayenne was speaking again, so Juni shook his bumming thoughts from his head and returned his attention to the interview.

"Well, I'm afraid your computers will be of no

help to you on *Power Trip*," Cayenne said chirpily. "But these parachutes sure will be!"

She handed each spy a heavy backpack. "Put these on immediately, please," she said.

Hurriedly, Juni hauled the backpack onto his shoulders and buckled it into place. Then he grabbed his other backpack full of gadgets and clipped it to his belt. The rest of the family suited up, too, glancing at one another with alarm in their eyes.

"Ready?" Cayenne said. She buckled a seat belt around her own waist. "Okay! It's time to show you the true meaning of the words *Power Trip*! As they say, bon voyage!"

With that, one of the producers threw open the airplane's hatch. The four spies were sucked out into the sky!

# CHAPTER 4

"**A**AAAAAHHHHHHH!" all four Cortezes hollered as they plummeted through the sky. Then they reached for their parachutes' rip cords and gave them mighty pulls.

*Thwoop! Thwoop! Thwoop! Thwoop!*

"Aaaah," all four Cortezes sighed as their free fall became a free float. When they had caught their breath, they looked at one another through the clouds.

"That was a little rude, don't you think?" Mom said to her family. "I mean, I like a nice sky dive as much as the next spy, but you kind of want to be prepared for it!"

"I have a feeling it's going to be hard to prepare for anything *Power Trip* has to throw at us," Carmen said with a sigh. "Speaking of which, uh, does anybody see any land down below?"

The family peered down past their toes. All they saw was beautiful, bright blue water.

"Okay . . ." Dad said hesitantly. "Tell me Juni, would it be good for ratings if we all perished at sea?"

"Actually," Juni said, biting his lip, "it might!"

"Hey, I see something!" Carmen blurted. She pointed down at the turquoise ocean. A giant white arrow made of plastic sheeting was floating on the gentle waves.

"It's pointing northeast," Juni said, consulting the compass on his spy watch with a grin. Juni just *loved* his spy watch. It was a computer, satellite mapping system, e-mail center, walkie-talkie, and lots of other cool devices, all in one. *And* it was waterproof. No Spy Kid should ever be caught without his or her spy watch. That's why Carmen and Juni *never* took theirs off.

"I estimate we've got about forty-five seconds before we hit the water," Juni warned his family.

"Just great," Carmen complained. "Forty-five seconds before our parachutes drag us beneath the surface like stones."

"You make a good point, Carmenita," Dad said. He began loosening his parachute's buttons and buckles. "Let's all get ready to ditch these chutes as soon as we touch down."

"And then what?" Juni wondered.

"We head northeast!" Dad said. "Good thing marathon swimming is part of the OSS training regimen."

"Yeah," Carmen said skeptically. "But at least when we swam the English Channel, we knew what to expect. Here, we have no idea how far we'll have to go—oh!"

*Splash!*

Carmen hit the sea, skimming across it like a skipping stone. The rest of the Cortezes touched down nearby. They quickly discarded their parachutes and watched them sink into oblivion. Dad took Juni's spy bag and slung it onto his own back. Then the entire family began swimming in the direction of the floating arrow.

They made swift progress. The water was warm and pleasant. Everything was going great until, suddenly, the waves started to get choppy.

Then it got rough.

Soon, the Cortezes were struggling against full-blown breakers! When they heard a great, syncopated roar above their heads, they knew the cause.

"Helicopter!" Carmen cried. She swiped a hank of salt-saturated hair out of her eyes and looked up. She gasped when she saw an MYPQ logo on the copter's tail. A cameraman on a tether was leaning out of the bird, filming the spies' every stroke.

"Okay. So far," Carmen announced, "I really hate being on a reality TV show."

"I'd love to say something to cheer you up, honey," Mom said, "but actually, I think it's only going to get worse!"

Mom lifted a trembling hand out of the water and pointed over her daughter's shoulder. Carmen, Dad, and Juni spun around and gasped. They were facing about fifty transparent, blobby bubbles, floating on the ocean's choppy surface. The blobs were heading straight for the spies.

"Jellyfish!" Juni cried. "The *Power Trip* producers must have planted them!"

Juni twisted in the water to face his family.

"So, here's the question," he said seriously. "Fight or flight?"

"Flight! Flight!" Mom, Dad, and Carmen cried together. Frantically, they began swimming away from the jellyfish, which simply bobbed serenely after them.

"C'mon, slowpoke!" Carmen cried, glancing over her shoulder at her brother. "Have you ever *felt* a jellyfish sting?"

"Have you?" Juni retorted.

"No, and I don't plan to start on TV!" Carmen

yelled, pointing up at the helicopters. She spat out a mouthful of salt water defiantly.

"Carmen," Juni shouted over the waves. "We're being taped. We're not actually on TV . . . yet! And if we win the game and expose the Cheathams as evil, the show will probably never air at all!"

"Hey, good point!" Carmen said, grinning at her brother. "Okay, I'm listening."

"But now *I'm* bummed!" Juni said morosely. It wasn't until that moment that he'd realized saving the world meant giving up his dreams of TV fame and fortune!

"Juni, might I remind you that an army of jellyfish is gaining on us with each passing second?" Carmen said. She splashed some seawater at her brother. "*And* we have a world to save? Get with the program! What's the plan?"

"Yes, Junito," Dad said. He and Mom had just doubled back to see what their Spy Kids were up to. "You're the TV expert. What are these *Power Trip*pers doing?"

"I think they're testing us," Juni said. "These reality shows are all about pointless bravery. You're rewarded for taking ridiculous risks. The grosser, the better."

"That's crazy!" Mom, Dad, and Carmen cried.

"That's reality TV," Juni declared.

"All right, then," Carmen said morosely. "We fight the jellyfish."

Giving the thundering helicopter a baleful glare, Carmen suddenly dove beneath the water. Surfacing right in front of one of the jiggly jellyfish, she whacked at the creature with a resounding karate chop.

The jellyfish quivered. And it quaked. It seemed to take a deep breath, puffing up until it was twice its size.

Then it raised a tentacle out of the water and spat at Carmen, hitting her with a stream of purple . . . jelly! The goop hit her with such force that she was hurled thirty feet through the water.

"Hey!" Dad cried. "Nobody slimes my little girl and gets away with it."

He lunged at the jellyfish. No sooner had he gotten near it, than he, too, was hit with a jet of jelly. Before he knew it, he was floating next to his daughter. And about six other jellyfish were swimming toward them—fast! Before they could even put up their dukes, Dad and Carmen were pummeled with great geysers of jelly, from purple to red to orange. The force carried them another fifty feet northeast.

"Hey," Carmen said, smacking her lips as she

wiped off her purple-smeared face. "This is *grape* jelly! Kinda tasty, actually!"

"See!" Juni called out. "We're being rewarded for our bravery. These aren't stinging predators. They're jelly-spewing jellyfish. And they're our ticket to shore. Not to mention, a snack!"

Juni crowed with delight as a stream of raspberry jelly hit him in the belly, carrying him a hundred feet through the water.

"Well, I guess we should just relax and enjoy the ride then," Mom said, just before a jellyfish propelled *her* forward with a stream of apricot jam.

"Mom!" Carmen shrieked as she was hit with another jet of superjelly. "I wouldn't exactly call this relaxing."

"No," Juni yelled as he whooshed through the water past his sister. "But it's fast! And check it out! Land ho!"

Juni was right! Up ahead, they could now see an island! It had everything a tropical island should have: a long stretch of sandy white beach; a lush forest of coconut palms and banana trees; a tall cliff with a bubbling waterfall. Further inland, the spies spotted some craggy mountains and even an overgrown pyramid built by some ancient natives.

After a lot more jelly blasts, the Cortezes

reached the shore. They crawled up on the beach, spitting out mouthfuls of salty jelly. They were sticky. And sandy. They looked completely gross. But they'd made it!

Naturally, three cameramen wearing backward baseball caps were there to capture it all. While two of the cameras zoomed in on Mom's tangled red curls and Carmen's sand-scraped knees, the third focused on a man, standing just clear of the surf. He was wearing spotless khaki shorts and sporty sandals. He gave his camera a toothy white smile and lifted a microphone to his lips. Then he sauntered over to the Cortezes.

"And *here* they are," the man announced. "Our challengers, the Cortez family! Welcome to Abeja Island. I'm your host, Jack Crakst. How does it feel to be on *Power Trip*, folks?"

"Sticky!" Carmen growled. "And hey, why are we the challengers, already? The game hasn't even begun yet."

"Oh, but it has!" Jack declared. His tanned face beamed and his sandy hair glistened in the sun. "Talk about a coincidence. When the Cheathams were dropped out of *their* plane, they just happened to have an inflatable motorboat in their gear bags. They got here hours ago."

Jack pointed a sinewy forearm across the beach. There were the Cheathams, lounging artfully on a blanket beneath a palm tree. They were wearing crisp white clam diggers and stylish, linen shirts. The mom, Margarita, wore a bright hibiscus blossom in her shiny black locks. The youngest Cheatham, Tate, was building an architecturally stunning sand castle. They were all nibbling the last bits of a delicious-looking lunch.

"The winners of the first *Power Trip* challenge," Jack continued, "the Cheathams, were awarded with a lovely luau."

"So, we don't get anything to eat!?" Juni gasped. "But I'm *staarrrving*!"

"Oh, that's terrible," said Allie, jumping to her feet. She flashed the camera a compassionate (and utterly fake) smile. "Please, come help yourselves to some of our food."

The Cortezes padded across the sand to eye the Cheathams' leftovers. There were a few suckling-pig ribs left; some melon rinds; the end pieces of a loaf of crusty bread. It wasn't exactly a generous offer. But what choice did they have? They couldn't win on *Power Trip* on completely empty stomachs. So, they shrugged and fell hungrily upon the dregs of the Cheathams' picnic.

As Carmen ate, she felt Allie staring at her. Carmen looked up from her bread crust in time to catch the other girl looking her up and down deliberately. Then Allie sniffed in derision.

The bread turned to sawdust in Carmen's mouth. She began to seethe quietly with rage.

Meanwhile, the grown-ups chatted politely.

"Enjoy the spread, old sport," Rich Cheatham said. He clapped Dad on the back. Hard. "We won't let this little game get personal, will we? Honor first, I always say. I have my great-uncle—the senator—to thank for that valuable lesson. Of course, those of us whose families *aren't* in the world-saving business might not understand."

Dad dropped the melon rind he was gnawing on. A growl rumbled deep in his chest. He turned to Rich Cheatham. *He* could tell him a thing or two about the world-saving business, all right. . . .

Suddenly, Mom poked Dad in the ribs.

"Remember our cover, honey," she whispered. "We're just computer consultants. Don't lose your temper!"

Dad swallowed hard. Of course, Mom was right. With great effort, he clamped his mouth shut. That is, until he felt something tugging at his jellied hair. When he glanced up, he discovered eight-year-old

Tate molding his sticky locks into a ridiculous mohawk!

"Hey!" Dad said, trying to maintain his dignity.

"Oh, don't worry, *Grrrrregorio*," Margarita said. "You look *darrrrling*. It's we women who will have a hard time looking pretty on camera. After all, we're not allowed to use any hair products or makeup."

"What?!" Mom squeaked. She eyed Margarita's long, long eyelashes suspiciously. Then she tried, in vain, to wipe her own face clean of jellyfish goop.

"But *you*," Margarita continued, staring at Dad and ignoring Mom. "You look fabulous as you arrrre. So *swarrrrthy* and . . . Spanish."

"Hey!" Now it was Mom who was growling—in jealousy. In fact, she seemed to be forgetting all about that "don't blow our cover" thing. But before she had a chance to give Margarita a piece of her mind, Jack Crakst's cheery voice jolted her out of her fury.

"Okay, contestants," he said. "Luxury time's over. Let's get right to your very first challenge!"

# CHAPTER 5

The Cheathams sprang to their feet. They were well fed and rested—not to mention totally photogenic. They were ready for anything.

But the spies were glancing at one another nervously. They had to launch into the contest already? They hadn't even had time to gather their spy gadgets! Juni was clutching his still growling stomach. Dad was trying to comb the silly mohawk out of his sticky hair. Mom and Carmen were still blinking jelly and salt water out of their red-rimmed eyes.

The spies were definitely not on their A-game.

But Jack Crakst took no notice. He simply raised his microphone to his chap-free lips and began rattling off a speech.

"Folks, we're just moments away from launching our exciting new show, *Power Trip*! And the challenge will be . . . a jungle obstacle course!" he said. "But first, let's make sure our contestants understand the rules."

Jack tossed each dad a fuzzy roll of palm-tree bark. The scrolls were scrawled with many paragraphs of fine print. Juni peeked over his dad's shoulder at the paper. It smelled fishy!

"The rules are written in squid ink!" he realized. "Wow, they're really trying to be authentic here."

"You can read those later when you've set up camp," Jack said with a good-natured chuckle. "For now, I'll just fill you in on the basics. *Power Trip* is all about points. With each challenge, you'll score points for how far ahead you finish, how creatively you rise to the challenge, and how fabulous you look while you play."

"Huh?!" the four Cortezes blurted.

Over in the cluster of Cheathams, Allie tossed her glossy hair over her shoulder and murmured, *"No problemo!"*

"Now a misstep will cost you three points, but a leg up will gain you four," Jack said quickly. "Tools are allowed, but you'll be penalized for them. And cheating is, of course, cheating! Curse words cost one point each. We'll be hearing a lot of those when you get to the more difficult challenges, I assure you!"

Jack winked at the camera.

"Now, docked points could cost you food, water,

or shelter," Jack continued. "It just depends on the time of day. Speaking of the time of day, the family with the highest grade-point average at two o'clock in the afternoon each day gets—you guessed it!—an extra point! And it's as simple as that. Everyone got it?"

"Uh . . ." Juni said, staring at the host. "Could you repeat the question?"

"That host is as cracked as his name!" Dad whispered to Mom and Carmen. "And these rules are a bunch of—"

"Gregorio!" Mom gasped. "Watch it. You don't want to get docked for a curse word before we've even begun."

"Mom, don't sweat it," Carmen whispered. "You heard what Jack said. The first challenge is an obstacle course. You know how many of those we had to do at OSS boot camp. We'll beat those softie Cheathams easy."

Mom peered down the beach at the beginning of the course. It was typical TV fare—twin arrangements of tires arranged in double rows, and ropes swinging over sinkholes.

"I'm sure you're right, honey," she whispered.

"Of course, she is," Juni piped up. He'd joined the family huddle. "You know, you almost gotta feel sorry for the Cheathams. They have no idea they're up against highly trained spies."

"I will never feel sorry for mind-manipulators," Carmen said, crossing her arms defiantly over her chest. Then she spun around and faced the *Power Trip* host.

"We're ready, Jack," she announced. "Let's get this show on the road."

"Tee-hee," Allie said, pointing at Carmen. "Look at her, trying to act all grown-up when she's only twelve. Isn't it cute?"

"Ex-CUSE me?" Carmen started to say. "Do you even *know* the meaning of the word Level One security clear—"

"Carmen!" Juni cried, cutting his sister off before *she* blew their cover. He shot the Cheathams a fake grin. "My sister—always daydreaming. She wants to be a spy, you know."

"How *drrrrroll*," Margarita said. "A child spy. Ha!"

"Let's just get this over with," Carmen grumbled. With her family, she stalked to the beginning of the obstacle course. Jack was waiting for them.

"Now," he said with a sunny smile, "you must cross over every single obstacle in order to win. This course will take you all the way through the jungle. And what reward will you find at the end? Your campsites! The winners will also find the fixings for a gourmet meal. The losers—a dull machete and hookless fishing pole."

"Okay, now we have *extra* incentive to win," Carmen muttered.

"All right," Jack said. "Only two people from each team will be allowed to compete. Choose your players."

The Cortezes glanced at one another.

"The jungle looks pretty dense," Mom observed. "The smaller, the better."

"You said it," Juni said. "Carmen and I will take this one."

"And when you get to the end," Mom said, chucking Juni under the chin, "your Dad and I will cook up that gourmet dinner!"

"Good luck, my Spy Kids," Dad said. He tousled Carmen's hair affectionately. Then he grimaced and wiped a palmful of jelly and sand on his shirt.

Carmen and Juni moved to their starting line. Nearby, Rich and Allie stepped up to their obstacle course.

"Letting your children fight your fight for you?" Rich called out to Dad. He started to raise his eyebrows in disapproval, but then he nodded. "Oh, I get it. You're teaching them some sort of lesson. Fine parenting, old chap!"

Dad glowered at Rich. "Why, you—"

"Believe me," Carmen interrupted quickly. She didn't want Dad to cost them points before they'd even begun! "My dad knows a ton about parenting. Watch and learn, Mr. Cheatham."

"Thanks, sweetheart," Dad whispered.

"As Allie would say," Carmen replied with a grin, *"no problemo!"*

Carmen returned her attention to Jack. The host raised his hand dramatically.

"Ready . . ." he began.

"You bet I am," Allie said. She shot Carmen a glare. Then she turned to a nearby camera and smiled sweetly.

"Set . . ." Jack continued. "GO!"

Carmen and Juni launched into the course. They hopped breezily through the rows of tires and swung over the sinkhole as lightly as cats. By the time they'd vaulted over a fallen palm tree and tunneled through a hollow log, they'd left Rich and Allie in the dust. They pressed on, plunging into the thick jungle. A cameraman, of course, was right on their heels.

"Ha!" Juni cried as he led the way down a

cramped trail. "This is a piece of cake! We're so gonna win this thi-ING! Oof!"

No sooner had Juni's boast left his lips than he'd tripped! He was stunned to find himself on the ground, buried in a bunch of ferns.

"Juni!" Carmen cried as she almost trampled her brother. "You're such a klutz. C'mon."

"I tripped on a root," Juni defended himself. "The foliage is so thick around here, you can't even see the ground!"

Carmen grabbed Juni's hand and tried to haul him to his feet. But his foot wasn't budging. In fact, something was hanging onto Juni's ankle! And it was starting to squeeze!

"Uh, Carmen," he quavered. "Maybe that *wasn't* a root."

He pawed at the ferns until he uncovered his leg. Then he screamed!

"It's a boa constrictor!" he cried. He pointed at a long, snaky, green thing wrapped around his ankle.

Carmen gasped. But then she took a closer look.

"Hello!" she sputtered. "It's a harmless vine that got wrapped around your ankle. You know, you're totally gonna flunk biology when you get to high school."

Carmen reached down to untangle the vine from Juni's leg. But before she could make any progress, another vine sprang from the ground. This one looped itself around her wrist!

"Aaaaaah!" the Spy Kids cried.

"The vines are alive," Juni shrieked.

Suddenly, the camera-ready face of Jack Crakst popped through the leaves of a nearby bush. He peered over at Carmen and Juni, as more vines began snaking themselves around their limbs.

"The vines are indeed alive, young Johnny," Jack announced.

"That's Juni!" Juni scowled. "J-U-N— mmmmmpph!"

Before he could finish spelling, a vine had curled around Juni's mouth!

Jack ignored Juni and spoke breathlessly into the TV camera.

"The Cortez kids have stumbled into a little obstacle we like to call . . . the Sargasso Swamp," he explained. "Let's see if they can get out of it!"

As quickly as he'd appeared, Jack ducked back into the foliage, leaving Carmen and Juni to fend for themselves. They were now completely ensnared by the hard-squeezing vines.

"Ooof," Carmen huffed to her brother. "My

arms are pinned. We have no gadgets, and I can't do any martial arts in this vine's kung fu grip. We've got nothing to work with here!"

"Mmmmmffff!" Juni grunted, his eyes bulging in fear.

Carmen tried to blow a hank of hair out of her eyes so she could think. But the hair didn't budge.

"Darn this jellyfish jelly!" she said. "I can't think when I'm so gummed up . . . hey!"

Suddenly, Carmen stopped complaining.

And then she started whistling! She twittered and clucked and whistled some more.

Now, Juni's eyes were bulging in disbelief. What was Carmen doing? Was this any time for bird calls?! Suddenly, though, Juni heard something echoing in the distance. He cocked his head.

*Twitter, twitter, cluck, whistle!*

Those were the exact same twitters, clucks, and whistles Carmen had just made! But this time, they were coming from the jungle!

Before Juni could put two and two together, an entire flock of tiny white birds broke through the trees! They flew straight to the Spy Kids and began pecking at them!

"MMMMMMMMM!" Juni shrieked from behind his vine.

"Relax," Carmen said. "They're Abeja Argots. They're sweet little birds—literally! They subsist on sugary berries, fruits, and, for our purposes, jelly!"

Carmen was right! The birds were giddily nibbling at the sugar-smeared spies. And in the process, their sharp beaks were slicing right through the sargasso vines. In only seconds, the Spy Kids were free!

"Whoo-hoo!" Juni cried as they scrambled out of the Sargasso Swamp.

The kids rushed back into the obstacle course. Now they were being chased by both the cameraman *and* the flock of Abeja Argots. But they paid their followers no mind. They had a race to win!

They plunged through a waterfall. They scrambled up a rock wall and down a gorge. Next there was a mud slick. And then after that—a nasty little obstacle called the Dung Beetle Dodge.

But finally, they spotted the finish line. And waiting for them on the other side were . . . Rich and Allie?!

"No!" Juni shouted.

Yes. The Cheathams had totally trounced the Spy Kids. Carmen and Juni slumped over in exhaustion and defeat. To make matters worse, two TV cameras swept in to film them while they lurched across the finish line. As a final insult, Jack Crakst popped up before them, oozing compassion.

"Now, here's a girl who takes her obstacle course seriously," he said to Carmen. "If I'm not mistaken, dear, you are caked in jelly, sand, leaves, bird feathers, mud, and dung. Pee-ew! I'm afraid that's gonna cost you a few aesthetic points."

Allie giggled and flipped her hair—which was still remarkably clean—over her unsullied shoulder.

"Plus," Jack added, "you and Juni finished a full half hour behind Rich and Allie."

"What?!" Juni yelled. "How?"

"Can you believe my Allie found us a shortcut?" Rich said with an innocent shrug. "A nice little rope bridge that went straight through the jungle. We had a smashing view from up there!"

"That's cheating!" Carmen cried. "You didn't go through the obstacles."

Jack shook his head sympathetically and snapped his fingers at one of the cameramen. The crew member hooked his camera into a small monitor. Then he played back a scene from the beginning of the course. In it, Jack was explaining the rules:

"You must cross over every single obstacle in order to win," he said, flashing a toothy smile.

The screen went blank. Then the real-life Jack spoke.

"You see?" he said. "Technically, Rich and Allie did go *over* every obstacle."

"Which means, *technically*," Allie said with a sneer in her voice, "it looks like the Cortezes will be fishing for their supper with a hookless pole! *Bon appétit,* Carmen and Juni!"

# CHAPTER 6

JACK CRAKST: Hello, folks. Jack Crakst here on the set of *Power Trip* on beautiful Abeja Island. We're approaching the campsite of Team Cortez. As you can see, there are straw pallets for sleeping. A tin bucket for both washing and cooking. And of course, the dull machete and hookless fishing pole. Yet, the mood here seems to be dark and stormy. You see, Carmen and Johnny—

JUNI: It's Juni. JUNI!

JACK: Uh-huh, kid. We're taping here—could you get out of my shot, please? As I was saying, the Cortez kids just suffered a humiliating defeat by Rich and Allie Cheatham. Let's get their postmortem. Carmen?

CARMEN: Not now, Jack. I'm trying to de-jell here.

JACK: Oh-kay, *somebody's* a little cranky. Must be a teen thing. Let's check in with little Johnny. Johnny? What happened out there today?

JUNI: What can I say, Jack? If I say the Cheathams cheated, I look like sour grapes. If I say, "Hey! You can't catch a fish with a hookless pole!" I look like a whiner. All I can say is, I'm proud to be on TV!

CARMEN: Gee, now you sound like a brownnoser.

JUNI: Shut! Up!

JACK: Fight! Fight! Fight!

CARMEN: . . . Uh, we're not fighting, Jack.

JACK: Oh . . . what a shame. But still! The mood at Camp Cortez continues to be very, very dark. Dark and stormy . . .

An hour after he'd arrived at Team Cortez's campsite, Jack Crakst finally decided he had enough humiliating footage. He and his cameraman left to go check on the Cheathams.

"I bet *they* happened to bring a nice, comfy trailer to sleep in," Carmen said, glancing bitterly around the bare-bones campsite. "Just by coincidence, of course!"

"Don't forget, sweetie," Mom said, "we have a few tricks up our sleeve as well. Spy gadgets! And now that the camera's gone, we can break 'em out."

Eagerly, the spies gathered around their gear bag. Juni unzipped it.

"I know we've got an Insta-Tent in here," he said excitedly. "And an iceless ice-cream maker! The freeze-dried food was probably ruined by the salt water, but with Uncle Machete's Nut 'n' Berry Detector, we can probably find some decent grub."

"Are there any hair-care products in there?" Carmen asked breathlessly.

"Carmen, how many times do I have to tell you?" Juni said. "Nobody's gonna see this show. So stop obsessing about how you look!"

"I meant for the fishing pole, doofus!" Carmen growled. "If we have a bobby pin, we could make it into a fishhook."

"Oh," Juni said. "Good idea. Let's see . . ."

He opened the bag wide and peered inside. Then he gasped in horror.

"No!" he cried.

"What is it?" Dad said. "Are the air mattresses punctured? Is our mini–satellite TV on the fritz?"

Juni didn't respond. He merely pulled a slip of paper out of the bag and read out loud: "'Dear Team Cortez. Sorry about this, but you're only allowed one "luxury item" while you're playing

*Power Trip.* We left you the freeze-dried food and confiscated everything else. It will be returned to you at the end of the game, of course. Your gracious host, Jack Crakst.'"

Juni pulled two handfuls of freeze-dried food packets from the bag. They were completely soaked with fishy-smelling ocean water.

"Nooooo!" he cried. "I'm starving. What do we do now?"

"Sweetie," Mom said cheerfully, "we don't need our gadgets to survive. We've got our wits! Now why don't you and I start building a shelter with some palm leaves. Dad and Carmen can go get us some dinner. There are some banana and coconut trees nearby. And look . . ."

Mom tore a corner off one of the aluminum food packets and twisted it into a pointy hook.

"See?" she said. "Fishhook."

"You are a brilliant woman, Ingrid," Dad breathed as he tied the fishhook to his line.

"Thanks, honey," Mom said. She walked to the edge of the beach and began to pull huge, spiky palm stalks out of the brush. As she worked, she glanced over her shoulder at her family. "I'm just thinking like a spy. As it says in the OSS manual, 'A good spy always keeps her eyes and ears op—'"

"Umm . . . speaking of which," Carmen interrupted, "look out, Mom!"

Mom turned back around just in time to duck. A dozen pointy palm leaves had just shot out of the branch she was holding! One of them missed her nose by a hair!

"Whoa!" Mom shrieked, falling backward into the sand. When she dropped the palm stalk, another barrage of leaves zinged out at her. Luckily, these spiky weapons missed her, too. Mom scooted backward until she was out of leaf-shot. Dad helped her to her feet.

"Shooting palm leaves don't occur in nature," Juni fumed. "That must have been another *Power Trip* challenge."

"Well, that was a dangerous one," Dad said. "They could have put someone's eye out."

"Okay, then," Mom said with a shrug. "I guess we don't *really* need shelter. This is a tropical island, after all! We can sleep beneath the stars. It'll be fun."

"You're right, we don't *need* shelter. But we *do* have to eat," Carmen said. She looked around hungrily. Then she pointed down the beach. "Hey, look! I see some ripe bananas on that tree!"

Carmen darted to the tree and used her

OSS-honed gymnastics skills to shinny up its trunk. She pulled a big bunch of bananas off a branch and brought it back to the family. Panting with hunger, Juni tore open one of the bananas. He was just about to take a huge bite of the fruit when Carmen screamed.

"Juni, don't!"

"Why not?!" Juni protested. Then he looked down at his dinner—and screamed himself!

"That's no banana!" he yelled. "That's a banana *slug*!"

It was indeed—a giant, slimy, bright yellow slug! Shooting Juni a, well, sluggish stare, the critter slithered out of its banana peel and into the sand with a plop. Then it undulated toward the trees.

"You know," Carmen said, tossing her own banana onto the beach in disgust. "I don't think these are *Power Trip*'s booby traps. It's the Cheathams! Remember what they said on the Cayenne Coyer show? They have a vineyard in northern California!"

"And . . . ?" Juni said, staring at his sister blankly.

"There's only one place in the world you find these kinds of banana slugs—in northern California," Carmen declared. "The Cheathams are trying to sabotage us!"

"Well, they're doing a pretty good job," Juni said, clutching his gut. "If I don't get something to eat soon, not only will I not be able to spy, I just might die!"

Mom's face darkened. She was a high-powered international superspy. She had saved the world dozens of times. She was tough as nails. But there was one thing she *couldn't* take, and that was her children going hungry!

With a determined grimace, Mom grabbed the fishing pole away from her husband.

"Honey," she declared. "I'll be right back. Can you start a fire, please?"

Dad gathered some driftwood and aimed his tooth laser beam at it. The wood burst into flames.

Minutes later, Mom strode out of the surf, bearing two heaping handfuls of sunfish.

"Ha!" she said defiantly. "Good thing they taught us fly-fishing at OSS boot camp."

Mom tossed the fish onto the fire. Before long, the Cortezes were happily devouring a basic—but yummy—barbecue.

Carmen tossed her fish bones into the fire. With her stomach full, her spy instincts were renewed. And they were focused on the Cheathams.

"I say we pay our competition a little visit—

undercover," she said, jumping to her feet and giving her brother a determined look. "The next time they pull a prank, I want to be ready for it."

Half an hour later, the Spy Kids reached the edge of the Cheathams' campsite. They burrowed beneath some giant ferns and peeked out at the scene. Carmen had to stifle a gasp.

"They're living in the lap of luxury!" she whispered angrily.

Juni could only nod and stare furiously at the Cheathams' posh campsite. At its center was a sprawling ranch house constructed of bamboo poles and woven straw mats. Rich was napping in a hammock in front of the house, and Margarita was swimming in a nearby babbling brook, complete with a little pool that hissed and bubbled like a natural Jacuzzi.

A bamboo table set up on the beach was just about groaning with tropical fruits, coconut-scented rice, steamed lobsters and clams, even frothy juice drinks with little paper umbrellas in them! For dessert, there was a platter of starfish-shaped chocolates.

"This is *so* not a fair fight," Carmen hissed to Juni. "Something fishy's going on. Let's get a closer look and see if we can figure out how they got all this stuff. Maybe they paid off some of the crew!"

"Gotcha," Juni said as Carmen ducked into the brush ahead of him. "There's definitely something . . . fishy . . . starfishy. . . ."

Before Juni could follow his sister, his eyes drifted to the plate of chocolates. Even though it was twenty feet away, Juni was sure he could smell the candy. In fact, that's *all* he could smell. All he could think about! He *had* to have some chocolate!

Before he could think twice, Juni was pressing a secret and seldom used button on his spy watch. A foot-long propeller popped out of the watch and began spinning with a low hum. That's when Carmen reappeared.

"What are you doing launching your emergency helicopter attachment?" she hissed. "You start flying and we'll get caught instantaneously."

"Didn't you read our spy watch's instruction book?" Juni asked with a giggle. "This baby's not just for flying. It's also a whiz at tunneling!"

"Juni, no!" Carmen whispered.

But Juni could not ignore the call of the chocolate. He thrust his propeller at the ground. Almost immediately it began burrowing into the sand, creating a perfectly round tunnel. Juni skittered after the propeller. He was underground!

In no time, he surfaced right below the Cheathams' table. He reached up and grabbed two handfuls of chocolates. Then he retraced his path back to Carmen's hiding place.

Or so he thought.

When his head popped up through the ground, he found himself under an unfamiliar banyan tree. Luckily, the tree was in the jungle and not in the middle of Camp Cheatham.

*Un*luckily, the tree was strung with a tire swing. And inside that tire swing was—Tate! He was staring down at Juni with an impish grin.

"Hello," he said, *"intruder!"*

# CHAPTER 7

"**T**ate!" Juni cried as he frantically collapsed his spy watch's propeller. He clambered out of the tunnel and tried to furtively stuff the chocolates into his cargo-pants pocket. "What are you doing here?"

"This is our camp," Tate said. He somersaulted out of his tire swing. Then he stalked up to Juni and planted his little fists on his hips. "The real question is, what are *you* doing here? Intruder!"

"Stop calling me that!" Juni said, stepping backward. "I have a perfectly good explanation for why I'm here, of course."

"Uh-huh."

"And that explanation is . . ." Juni said. He paused. He hoped the pause would seem dramatic. But in his heart, he knew it was just desperate.

"I was *digging*," Juni finally burst out.

"I can see that," Tate said, taking in the fresh dirt on Juni's already filthy clothes. "Digging for what?"

"Uh . . . grubs!" Juni burst out. "You know, I'm a scholar of reality TV, so I'll fill you in on a little secret—they *always* make you eat bugs. So . . . I thought I'd practice by snacking on some fresh creepy-crawlers. I guess I dug a little too far and ended up in your camp."

"Uh-huh," Tate said again. He cast a sly glance through the trees behind him. Juni followed his gaze. Tate was eyeing his snoozing dad and swimming mom.

No! Juni thought. He's gonna squeal!

"You think I'm gonna squeal, don't you?" Tate asked, turning back to Juni.

"No, of course not!" Juni said nervously.

"Tell you what," Tate said. "You give me half the candy you just stuffed in your pocket and I'll keep my mouth shut. Except to eat the candy, of course. My mom said I can't have any till after dinner. Which is, like, a whole hour from now! It's torture waiting for dessert, y'know?"

Oh, Juni knew, all right. He bit his lip. He hated to part with his hard-won chocolate. But a good spy had to make sacrifices. So, finally, he nodded and handed over half his loot.

"Thanks," Tate said, stuffing a starfish into his mouth. "So, where'd you get that propeller thingy?

It reminds me of the tunnel-shooter in my favorite video game, Gigantic Goobers from Outer Space."

"Gigantic Goobers from Outer Space?" Juni cried. "That's *my* favorite video game. What level are you up to?"

"Only fifty-six," Tate said morosely. "And I bet this week away is going to hurt my game."

"But you're on TV!" Juni said. "That's a pretty nice consolation, right?"

"I guess," Tate said with a shrug. "I'll be especially consoled when Jack Crakst wants to interview me. I've got a whoopee cushion and a stink bomb *allllll* ready!"

Tate started cackling so hard, he spewed chocolate on Juni's shirt. Juni couldn't help but giggle himself.

"Kid," he said, "I like the way you think."

"You know what else I'm thinking?" Tate said. "I found a great clam bed down the beach a ways. It's really fun to dig those little buggers out of the sand. If your timing isn't perfect, you could lose a finger or a toe!"

"Coooool," Juni breathed.

"Why don't you go clamming with me?" Tate offered. "You look pretty hungry. Besides, it's no fun clamming alone. And of course, Allie won't go with me. She's too busy making jewelry."

Jewelry! Juni thought in alarm. Like the evil Brain Beater bracelet!

A chill ran down Juni's spine, just as a solitary bird squawked ominously in the trees.

*Ca-CAW! Ca-CAW!*

Juni shivered. But then he quickly shook off his willies. He didn't have time for fear! He had some important spying to do!

"Clamming with you?" he said to Tate slyly. "Sounds perfect. Let's go!"

*Ca-CAW! CA-CAW! CA-CAW!*

"Whoa, that bird's wigging out," Tate said, peering into the dense foliage. Juni peered, too. And when he saw some leaves rustling about five feet off the ground, he got a sinking feeling in his gut.

"Uh, Tate," he said, "I'll be right back."

"Sure," Tate said, heading back toward Camp Cheatham. "I'll go get a bucket for the clams."

As soon as Tate was out of earshot, Juni plunged into the trees. Sure enough, his sister was lurking among the branches.

"Nice birdcall," Juni said. "Real subtle!"

"Well, I had to get your attention somehow," Carmen said. "Before you defected to the other side! Is Tate your best friend now?!"

"As if!" Juni retorted. "I'm spying! Although . . . I've got to admit, Tate is a pretty cool kid. I don't think he knows his family wants to take over the world. They probably haven't told him because he's so young and all."

"He's only two years younger than you," Carmen said with a sneer.

"Hey," Juni protsted. "Two years is a *lot*. It's like . . . 730 days! Anyway, I'll have the last laugh when I come back with all sorts of juicy intel. Not to mention . . . tomorrow's lunch!"

JACK: Hello, folks. Jack Crakst here at Camp Cheatham. Oh! And here's Allie Cheatham. It looks like she's making a bracelet. She's really embracing the whole desert-island, do-it-yourself thing. So, Allie, any thoughts on your competition?

ALLIE: What competition, Jack?

JACK: Ha-ha! I'm talking about the Cortezes.

ALLIE: Like I said, *what* competition? I mean, I'm sure they're a *very* nice family. But they're pretty rough around the edges, know what I mean?

JACK: It's true, Team Cortez isn't winning

many aesthetic points. But you never know. They might have a trick up their sleeve in the next challenge. It's a doozy! Hey, speaking of aesthetic points, what's that you're working on?

ALLIE: Just a little bracelet. Aren't the blue stones pretty?

JACK: They're . . . they're . . . *beautiful.*

ALLIE: I know, Jack. I know.

The next morning found the Cortezes sleeping fitfully in their shelterless campsite. They were all suffering as sand crept inside their pajamas, the early morning sunshine blazed through their eyelids, and the first tide crashed in their ears.

They were almost relieved when an alarm woke them up.

*Almost* relieved, because that alarm was Carmen—screaming.

"BUG! Bugbugbugbug!" she howled. *"Heeeeeelp! Get it off me!"*

Juni's eyes snapped open in time to see his sister hopping frantically around the beach. She was staring down at her pajama top and she was pale with fright.

"Man, Carmen," Juni said, hauling himself

painfully off his straw pallet. "For someone who just last month took out an anaconda with her bare hands, you sure are a fraidycat."

"You *know* I have a problem with bugs!" Carmen shrieked. "Besides, this thing's *huge*!"

"Uh-huh," Juni sighed. He ambled over to his sister. "Don't worry, I'll kill the itsy-bitsy spi—*aaaigh!*"

Juni spotted Carmen's bug. It was clinging mightily to her pajama top.

"That thing's huge!" Juni yelled. "It's a tarantula! Mom! Dad! *Heeeeelp!*"

"Who's a fraidycat, now?" Carmen said, sticking her tongue out at her brother. Then she resumed her trembling as their parents ran over in alarm. At first, Mom and Dad were horrified by the spider, too. But then, Dad leaned over for a closer look. He examined the tarantula carefully. Finally, he harrumphed and simply plucked it off Carmen's shirt.

"Aaaaah! Watch out!" the rest of the Cortezes shrieked.

"*Mi familia,*" Dad said with a grin. "It's not real. It's just a little robot, see?"

The other spies looked closely. Dad was right! The tarantula had metal hinged legs and flashing red eyes. It was almost cute!

Until, of course, it opened its mouth and spit out a gob of gooey paper.

"Gross!" Juni said.

"Hey wait," Carmen said, scooping up the paper. "There's writing on here."

She smoothed the note out on her leg and read:

*Time to take a Power Trip*
*    to Abeja's highest tip.*
*Get there first, plant your flag,*
*    and you'll be rewarded with plenty of swag,*
*        not to mention points galore.*
*Will you win the challenge . . . or*
*    will it be the Cheathams? Again!*

"The nerve," Mom said. "It's almost like they *want* the Cheathams to win."

"They're just baiting us," Juni said. "It's the way reality TV goes."

"Well, it's working!" Carmen said angrily. She crumpled up the poem and tossed it into the sand. Then she began typing into her spy watch.

"Highest tip, huh?" she said. She quickly patched into the watch's Topography Gauge. "Cinchy. It'll take my watch about five minutes to map out this entire island and tell us exactly where to go. Then we'll hit the trail. There's no way the Cheathams can get there first!"

# CHAPTER 8

**W**hile Carmen's watch buzzed and whirred through its calculations, the rest of the family gathered up gear for the hike. Mom plunged into the woods and picked coconuts, guavas, and mangoes from non-booby-trapped trees. Dad plucked everyone's clothes from the tree where they'd hung them to dry. And Juni peered into the bucket of clams he'd caught the day before with Tate. There was no time to steam them before the hike, so Juni simply poured the water out of the bucket, wrapped the clams in a plastic tarp, and stashed them in his backpack.

"Maybe when she's feasting on these tasty clams for lunch," Juni murmured, "Carmen will stop razzing me for not getting any dirt from Tate yesterday."

Juni sighed as he recalled the previous afternoon's events. Tate had spent the whole clamming trip talking about video games and dime-store gags.

He'd seemed like just an ordinary, innocent kid. Juni figured he'd been right—the rest of the Cheathams must have left Tate in the dark about their evil ways.

But at least he helped me catch these clams, Juni thought. Yum!

Carmen's voice jolted Juni from his shellfish daydreams.

"I've got a read," she announced. "Abeja's highest tip is a mountaintop about three miles away. We've got a long hike ahead of us. Let's go!"

JACK: And it looks like Team Cortez is on its way. Let's check in with them on the trail, shall we? *(Huff, puff!)* So, Carmen, your team figured out our clue pretty quickly—

CARMEN: Quicker than Team Cheatham?

JACK: Oh, I can't tell you that, young lady! But I can dock you a point for attempting to pilfer information from your host.

CARMEN: Doh!

JACK: Read the fine print, Miss Cortez. And while you're at it, you might want to run a comb through that hair. Speaking of bedhead, hey, Johnny! How was your first night camping out?

JUNI: Rustic, Jack. Really, rustic. Plus, two of our team's taller members were up late last night, whispering and totally keeping me awake. I think they may have been forming an alliance against me and Carmen.

GREGORIO: Junito! We're on the same team! Your mother and I would never—

JACK: Ah, tension. Warms my heart, it does. Oops, this hike's getting pretty steep. *(Huff, puff!)* I'll be doing the rest of this journey by helicopter. Smell ya later, Team Cortez. And I do mean *smell*!

An hour later, the spies were still climbing. The trail continued to get steeper. And rockier. Things were really on the verge of getting ugly. Juni had ripped the sleeves off his T-shirt and wrapped a *Power Trip* bandanna around his head. His eyes were feverish with competitive edge and hunger. Mom had been twisting her soft curls into dreadlocks as she hiked. Now her hair was sprouting from her head like wild vines. Dad had grown a bit withdrawn. Every once in a while, he began humming Spanish lullabies that he remembered from his childhood.

After a while, Juni spoke up.

"What're our coordinates?" he asked as he fought his way through a thicket of extrascratchy pricker bushes.

Carmen wiped the sweat off her face with her *Power Trip* bandanna and held up her spy watch. At the press of a button, a 3-D hologram of Abeja Island popped out of the watch and hovered around her wrist.

"We're really close!" she cried, pointing at the spies' location on the map. "In fact, according to this, we should be able to see our mountain right after we get through a rubber-tree grove up ahead."

"That's easy enough!" Juni cried. His energy was renewed. He began to trot down the trail with his family in tow. Soon, he saw a stand of trees whose leaves were round and bulbous.

"Hey," Juni cried over his shoulder as he kept running. "The watch was right on. Here's the rubber tree gro—"

*Sprroiiinnnngggg!*

"*Whooooa!*" Juni cried. He was flying backward through the air! He landed at his parents' feet with a grunt. This jolted Dad out of his Spanish lullaby.

"Son!" he cried. "What happened?!"

"I dunno," Juni said, shaking his head dully. "I guess I knocked into a rubber tree. A really *bouncy* rubber tree!"

Mom frowned and walked up to another tree. She swatted at its leaves.

*Sppprooooing!*

"*Aaaaaah!*" Mom screeched. She, too, was thrown backward through the air.

"The rubber trees are rigged," Dad growled as he helped Mom to her feet. "I guess we'll have to go around the grove."

Carmen checked her watch again.

"That'll add at least another hour to the trip," she complained. "Which will give the Cheathams a big enough window to win."

"If only we had our rocket shoes," Juni sighed. "Or our spring soles. Or our super pogo sticks . . ."

"Wait a minute," Carmen exclaimed suddenly. "We don't need those gizmos. With a little tinkering, we can turn these trees into trampolines! Watch!"

Carmen mopped her damp face with her bandanna again. Then she held the corners of the sweat-soaked fabric and stretched it up over her head. It looked like a boat's sail billowing out behind her.

Next, Carmen eyed a short rubber tree and began running toward it at high speed. She leaped at the tree. Her foot hit one of the megabouncy leaves and flung her upward.

Make that up, up, and away! Using her new bandanna/sail as a rudder, Carmen steered herself clear over the grove. She landed neatly on her feet just beyond the trees. When she looked around, she realized she was at the base of a tall, craggy mountain—*the* mountain they needed to climb to get to Abeja's highest point and win the challenge.

"Yes!" Carmen cried, pumping her fist.

"Carmen?! You okay?"

It was Mom's voice echoing through the walkie-talkie in Carmen's spy watch.

"Yup!" Carmen crowed into her own watch. "Hop on over. We're almost there!"

Uh, famous last words.

After they'd all sproinged over the rubber tree grove, the spies tethered themselves with harnesses and climbing ropes. They began scaling the mountain, which was actually more like a cliff—a sheer, very steep cliff with few fingerholds and tenuous toeholds.

The spies were in a spot!

"Good thing climbing Mount Everest is part of OSS boot camp," Dad grunted as he pulled himself up inch by painful inch.

"Just think of the view we'll have when we reach the top," Carmen groaned back. She was clinging to the cliff just above her Dad. "We can bask in our glory, sunbathe, and have a picnic lunch."

"Lunch!" Juni sighed. "Yum! I think I'll make us a nice clambake when we hit the top. And we can use my spy-watch propeller to whip up some tasty tropical fruit smoothies. . . ."

"Let's not count our curries before we've climbed," Mom warned Juni. "We've got a long haul ahead of us."

"And plus," Carmen pointed out with a note of alarm in her voice, "I think the clams might not be too happy about our plans for them. They're doing backflips in Juni's backpack!"

"Huh?" Juni gasped, glancing over his shoulder.

Carmen was right! His backpack was shuddering and shaking. He could feel the clams squirming around inside it.

"Whoa!" Juni cried. They were starting to squirm harder and harder! "Something's up with these clams!"

*Pow! Kerpow-pow-pow!*

"They're *blowing* up!" Carmen yelled. "That's what's up with them."

"Ew!" Juni shrieked as some exploded clam gunk hit him on the back of the neck.

"Uh, make that pee-ew, son," Dad said. "Those little buggers stink! Drop your pack!"

"I can't!" Juni cried. His fingertips were locked into two cracks in the mountainside. If he let go with even one of his hands, he'd fall off the cliff!

"Okay, we'll come to you and cut the backpack off," Mom said from her perch about ten feet away from her son. "Just hang tight, Juni. Literally!"

Juni clung to the cliff, fighting back the urge to throw up every time another stinky clam exploded in his pack. While he waited for his family to come to his rescue, he breathed through his mouth and plotted revenge.

"I can't believe I thought that Tate was innocent. *He* rigged these clams," Juni raged. "He's as deceptive as his dad and as sneaky as his sister. But just wait till he sees how I'm gonna get him back—"

"*Aaaaaigggggh!* Help!"

The four spies started. The voice had come from the other side of the mountain, somewhere below them.

Carmen flipped a small, extendable periscope

out of her spy watch and peered through it. She could just see around the mountain. . . .

"It's Allie!" she announced in surprise.

Make that Allie in serious trouble. In fact, she was dangling from a branch growing from the side of the cliff. If the flimsy twig broke, she was a goner! The family of spies looked at one another uncertainly. Allie sounded like she was in serious trouble.

*"Heeeeeeeelp meeeeee!"* she squealed. *"Pleeeease!"*

# CHAPTER 9

Carmen described Allie's precarious situation to her family. Then she looked from Juni's still spewing backpack to her teenage opponent, who was dangling from the branch, kicking frantically and screaming her head off.

"It could be a trap," Carmen said darkly. "Maybe the Cheathams faked Allie's fall to trip us up again."

"You're right," Juni said, wincing as another glob of clam guts hit him in the neck. "It might be just another ploy to win the competition."

As if to feed Juni's skepticism, another voice rang out from around the mountain. This time it was Rich.

"Help us!" he begged. "My daughter's in trouble. You can get to her more quickly. After all, we're much closer to the top than you."

"Gee, the guy really knows how to rub salt in the wound, doesn't he?" Carmen scowled.

Mom and Dad gave each other worried glances. But before they could say anything, Juni piped up quietly, "What if this isn't a ruse? What if Allie's really in trouble? Even if she is one of the bad guys, we've got to save her."

The entire family was silent for a moment. Then Dad said, "Juni, you're right. Our first priority should always be to help someone in need. I'm proud of you."

With that, the four Cortezes clustered together. They cut Juni's pack from his arms and emptied it of stinky clam bombs. Then, together, they edged their way around the mountain until they were only a few feet from Allie.

Holding one of the loose backpack straps himself, Dad tossed the other strap over to Allie. She grabbed it and hung on tight while Dad swung her to safety.

The moment Dad made the save, Jack Crakst's helicopter burst onto the scene and hovered next to the cliff. Crew members helped all five *Power Trip*pers climb from the mountain into the chopper. Then the bird shot up to the mountaintop.

Rich, Margarita, and Tate were waiting there, pale-faced and shaken. They'd even forgotten to plant their flag on the mountain's highest point!

When Allie climbed out of the helicopter, Margarita ran over to her.

"My darrrrrling," she cried. "I was so frrrrightened!"

An ashen Rich shook Dad's hand as the rest of the passengers stepped out of the helicopter.

"Mighty sporting of you, old sport," he said, "saving Allie like that. That was a close one!"

"Well, we Cortezes have a saying," Dad said. "Honor before mission."

Before Rich could reply, Jack signaled for the helicopter to turn off its roaring propeller. Then he lifted his microphone and began speaking breathlessly to one of the TV cameras.

"Jack Crakst here at the highest point on Abeja Island," he said, running a hand through his windblown locks. "As you've just seen, there's been a dramatic development. Dramatic indeed. Team Cheatham was on the very cusp of triumph. They were only seconds away from planting their flag on the mountaintop and winning the challenge when Allie stepped on a rock and tripped! On the sheer side of a cliff face, she clung to life by her very fingernails, I tell you. And then, Team Cortez came to her rescue! Such selflessness, such integrity!"

Jack placed a finger on one ear.

"Wait a minute, I'm getting an urgent dispatch from MYPQ's national headquarters," he said breathlessly. "Yes? Oh, my! But that's unheard of!"

Jack shook his head in awe and admiration and said to the camera, "Well, folks, to honor the Cortezes' noble deed, MYPQ's president has declared this challenge a draw! Of course, the Cheathams are still in the lead, fourteen points to six."

"How did he come up with that figure?" Juni whispered to Carmen.

"But still, the Cortezes are not losing nearly as badly as they were before," Jack continued. "It's truly an inspiring day here at *Power Trip.*"

"Well, I can't let the network president be the only one to extend gratitude," Rich said, stepping forward with a harrumph. "Gregory?"

"Gregorio," Dad said politely.

"Whatever," Rich said dismissively. "I'd like to invite you and your family to our camp tonight for a luau. It's the least we can do."

The spies regarded one another with raised eyebrows. They were all thinking the same thing: excellent spying opportunity! *With* dinner!

"You're on," Mom said, shooting Rich a friendly smile. "We'll see you at six." The two families smiled nervously at each other. Dinner was going to be interesting, to say the least.

JACK: Hi, folks, Jack Crakst here. As you can see, I'm all dressed up for tonight's big "burying-the-hatchet-at-least-for-one-evening" luau. Let's see how the Cortezes are do— Oh, my. You folks sure cleaned up good!

INGRID: Why, Jack, you sound surprised.

JACK: Is that an evening gown made of woven palm leaves, Ingrid?

INGRID: Uh-huh. I thought it made a certain . . . statement.

JACK: And look at Greg and Johnny in their muscle shirts and slicked hair.

JUNI: It's Juni, Jack. And we have the jellyfish to thank for this awesome hair gel.

JACK: Carmen, of course, is the coolest, in her grass skirt and halter. Oh, so tropical! I'm sure Allie will be *green* with envy. Ha! However did you pull this ensemble together?

CARMEN: It was nothing. After all, every sp—er, computer consultant—knows how to whip something up out of nothing.

JUNI: I just hope that isn't the case with tonight's dinner!

A short while after the obligatory Jack interview, the Cortezes walked confidently into their enemy's camp. They were pretty proud of their rustic-cool threads . . . until they got a load of the Cheathams' wardrobe. Somehow, their competitors had arrived on the island with perfectly pressed designer clothes! Margarita wore a silk gown and Allie wore supertrendy flares with a glittery halter top. Both Cheatham men wore linen blazers and Euro-chic sandals.

"Gee, *what* a coincidence," Carmen whispered to her brother dryly.

"Cortezes!" Rich Cheatham called. He bounded forward to hand coconut-shell cocktails to Mom and Dad. Then he flashed one of the ever-present TV cameras a sparkly smile. "Welcome, welcome, to our humble campsite. Have some of my famous coconut-rum punch."

"Humble?" Juni said, looking around the campsite in awe. It was even more lush than it had been the day before! A hammock was swinging gently between two palm trees. And a cameraman seemed to have been pulled into duty as a bartender/valet. He was mixing frothy fruit smoothies and pouring them into more coconut shells.

"So," Rich said kindly, looking the family up and down. "It seems you're still recovering from our little outing this afternoon. If you'd like to clean yourselves up a bit, you could use the freshwater shower we've rigged up over there."

Rich pointed to a luxurious outdoor bathroom at the far end of the camp.

"My wife spent all afternoon weaving that dress," Dad said, turning a bit red.

"Oh, don't worry, Gregorrrio," Margarita said, trotting over to the group and flashing Dad a sultry smile. "You look marrrrvelous. Don't change a thing!"

"Uh, that's *my* line," Mom said, shooting Margarita an edgy glare.

"What is that saying?" Margarita shot back with a glare of her own. "You snooze, you lose?"

"Heh-heh," Dad said awkwardly. "Ladies, ladies, I thought there were only *two* teenagers here tonight."

Allie chuckled. She was leaning against a nearby tree, nursing a strawberry smoothie. "Actually, Mr. Cortez, there's just one. After all, twelve does not a teenager make, does it?"

Carmen glared at Allie, who glanced at one of the TV cameras, which were swooping around the families like vultures. Batting her eyelashes, she confided to the world (or so she thought), "Carmen might not be very grown-up yet, but I'm sure she's a really *nice* person."

Carmen gasped in outrage. Allie was totally insincere. And manipulative. And mean! She was just pure evil!

This, Carmen thought wearily, is gonna be a long nigh—

*POW! Powpowpowpowpow!*

Everybody jumped. Something was exploding!

"Incoming!" Rich Cheatham cried. He grabbed his wife and daughter and pulled them into their bamboo bungalow. He slammed the door in the spies' faces.

Shut out of the shelter, the Cortezes could only hit the beach. They covered their heads with their hands.

"What's happening?" Carmen wondered breathlessly.

"And where's Juni!?" Mom cried.

Dad sniffed the air.

"Smell that?" he said. "Stink bombs!"

He hopped to his feet and strode into the trees

bordering Camp Cheatham. Sure enough, when he pulled back the leaves, he discovered Tate and Juni giggling over the stinky remains of several clam bombs.

"So, *that's* how you did it!" Juni was saying to the impish eight-year-old. "I gotta hand it to you, Tate. Even if you are a pain in the butt, you're a master mischief maker."

"And you," Dad said to Juni, "are in some major trouble, mister."

Despite the threat, a smile was tugging at the corners of Dad's mouth. Until, that is, Rich appeared at his side.

"Teaching my boy to make stink bombs, are you?" Rich said to Juni. "Well, what else could I expect from such a ruffian?"

"Ruffian?" Dad bellowed. "Maybe you and your family should look in the mirror, Cheatham!"

"Right back at you, Cortez," Rich replied, sniffing at Dad's slick hair and homemade threads. "Face it, sport. You're outclassed on this island. I think we *both* know who's going home with the Armadillo Wax."

Dad's hands clenched into fists.

His jaw went stony.

His brown eyes turned cold.

Juni held his breath. He'd never seen his dad this angry. He was going to beat Rich up! They'd be disqualified from *Power Trip* and the Cheathams would win! Nooooo!

"No," Dad said quietly, as if he'd somehow sensed Juni's silent panic. Instead of belting Rich, he merely gave him a dark scowl—a scowl filled with disdain, determination, and, most of all, honor.

"Thank you for the dinner invitation," Dad murmured. "But I'm afraid we have to leave now. You see, Cheatham, we have to get back to our camp to prepare."

"For what?" Cheatham asked lightly.

Dad glared at his foe. In a low growl, he answered, "War!"

# CHAPTER 10

The next morning, Juni was up with the sun. He walked up the beach and tentatively approached a fruit tree. When he was satisfied that it wasn't booby-trapped, he grabbed a couple of guavas from a low-hanging branch. Gnawing on the fruit, Juni ambled toward the water. He was kicking listlessly at the surf when he saw something glinty, bobbing on the waves nearby. It looked like a . . . bottle! It had a cork in it and Juni could see a note rolled up inside.

It's the classic message in a bottle! Juni thought. And only one person sends a message in a bottle—someone who's stranded on a remote island. Or drifting in an oarless rowboat. In other words, someone who's in big trouble!

As Juni's save-the-world instincts kicked in, he dropped his breakfast in the sand. He waded into the waves and made a grab for the bobbing bottle.

*ZZZZZZT!*

"Huh?" Juni blurted. The bottle had suddenly

zipped out of his reach! Now it was floating a good ten feet away.

Shrugging, Juni paddled after the bottle and reached for it again. But *again*, the bottle darted away! In fact, it seemed to be swimming. It was teasing him!

Juni gritted his teeth. He thought about the failed obstacle-course run. He thought about exploding clams and feuding families and squandered starfish chocolates. Then he let out a mighty roar and dove beneath the waves. He swam as hard as he ever had, darting beneath the bottle with the fleetness of a fish. Then he reached up and grabbed the thing!

*ZZZZZZzzzzzzz* . . .

The bottle's get-up-and-go died away. Howling in triumph, Juni splashed out of the waves. When he reached the shore, his parents and sister were running toward him in alarm.

"What happened!?" Carmen cried, blinking the last dregs of sleep from her eyes. Juni noticed that everyone was looking a little worse for the wear. Mom's dreadlocks were poking out in every direction, and Dad's five-o'-clock shadow was turning into a scruffy beard. But this was no time to worry about such trivial matters as that.

"What happened is an opportunity," Juni crowed. "We may be totally blowing this *Power Trip* mission, but we can still do some good. We can come to the rescue of whoever sent this message!"

"Juni," Mom said, gently prying the bottle from her son's grip. "We're not *blowing* this mission."

Carmen, Dad, and Juni gave Mom a skeptical gaze.

"Okay, so things aren't going so well," Mom admitted with a shrug. "But there's still hope. There *has* to be. Otherwise, the world as we know it is *doomed*."

Juni's shoulders slumped. He'd almost forgotten about this mission's high stakes and the evilness of Allie's Brain Beater. He'd forgotten about TV!

"Your mother is right," Dad said as Mom uncorked the bottle. "We have to focus. We have to formulate a detailed strategy of attack and counterattack. Without a well-thought-out plan, *we're* doomed."

"Uh . . . honey?" Mom said as she pulled the note from the bottle and gave it a quick read. "You might want to rephrase that. . . ."

Mom showed her family the scrap of paper. Juni scanned it quickly, his eyes widening as he read.

"It's not from a stranded sailor at all," he

exclaimed. Then he read the scrap of paper out loud:

> In an open space, glinting blue and green,
>> a treasure lies in a place unseen.
> Skitter-scamper to this goal,
>> and get there quick, before your foe.
> Is the find precious?
> No, it's not, until it's in a special slot.
> Only then, will you behold
>> clue number two, then off you'll go
>> on the second leg of this,
>> your topsy-turvy Power Trip.

Carmen sighed and said, "Doesn't it seem like there's an awful lot of bad poetry on our missions lately?"

"We don't have time to worry about presentation," Juni blurted. "This is a clue. And it's time-sensitive! We've gotta move!"

"Which means," Mom said to Dad regretfully, "I guess we're going to have to save our strategizing for some other time."

"All right," Dad said with a sigh. "Let's puzzle this out. We need to look for a treasure in an open space."

"A blue-and-green open space!" Carmen cried. "Easy enough—a field filled with blue wildflowers."

"Or a treetop in the sky," Juni proposed.

"Maybe it's a body of water," Mom argued.

"It could be anything!" Carmen realized. "Okay, let's consult my map again."

Carmen activated her hologram of Abeja Island. The spies studied it carefully. In the dense jungle that covered the island, there were only two gaps—a meadow hidden by a circle of trees and a wide, freshwater pond.

"Okay," Dad said. "We have two open spaces and four spies. I say we split up and check both of them out. Your mother and I will go for the pond. You kids check out the meadow. Who knows what this treasure might be."

"I do think it's safe to say it's not going to be pleasant," Carmen said grimly. She heaved a big sigh and said to her brother, "Let's get going. We can't afford to lose another point to those Cheathams."

An hour later, Carmen and Juni were approaching the meadow. It hadn't been an easy hike. First, they'd run into another thicket of superbouncy rubber trees. They'd successfully *sproing*ed over the grove, but they'd collected a few new cuts in the process.

Then they'd continued down the trail, until Juni had spotted a snack—a juicy, ripe mango—under a tree.

"Hey, I never *did* have breakfast this morning," he'd exclaimed. "What luck!"

"We don't have time to stop, Juni," Carmen called over her shoulder.

"I know," Juni said, scooping up the mango. "That's the beauty of fruit. It's a meal in the palm of your hand."

"It's official. You *do* watch too much TV," Carmen said. "You sound just like a commercial."

"Whatever," Juni said. He peeled the mango as he tromped down the trail. When the juicy flesh was revealed, he grinned and went in for a big bite.

"Owwwwww!" Juni bellowed. "I think I chipped my tooth!"

He gaped down at his mango. It had changed into a rock!

"That's no mango," Carmen huffed. She stomped back to Juni, grabbed the rock, and threw it into a nest of ferns. "It's a *chango*! They change into rocks to protect themselves from predators. Didn't you read the fine print?"

"Grrrr," Juni grumbled as he and Carmen

resumed their hike. ". . . Never get a decent meal . . . no fair . . ."

The trees were getting more sparse, and sun was dappling the Spy Kids' heads. But Juni was so disgruntled, he didn't even notice.

". . . Reality TV," he muttered. "Not all it's cracked up to be . . ."

"Shhh," Carmen admonished him suddenly. "We're here! In the meadow."

Juni peeked over Carmen's shoulder. They were looking at a sunny field surrounded by a circle of palm trees. The field was carpeted with strawlike sea grass and patches of sand. A few hermit crabs scuttled around the kids' shoes. But there were no other signs of life.

"I don't see any blue flowers," Juni whispered. "Or blue anything! Maybe this is the wrong place."

"Or maybe the treasure's blue," Carmen said. "Anyway, we might as well start searching."

The kids began walking around the field. They poked through the grass, peered behind palm trunks and pondered the poem in their minds. In fact, they were both thinking so hard, neither of them heard a scuffling, snorfling animal steal up behind Carmen. It wasn't until the animal was breathing down her neck that Carmen turned around.

She tried to scream. But she was so terrified no sound came out! She simply fell over in shock. She gazed up at the creature looming over her. It looked an awful lot like an iguana. The difference was, it was the size of a rhinoceros! The gigantic blue lizard was gazing at Carmen with calm, curious green eyes.

Carmen glanced over her shoulder scanning the area for her brother. There he was, on the other side of the meadow—and right in front of another giant iguana! He was just as oblivious to it as Carmen had been.

Finally, Carmen found her voice.

"Juni!" she shrieked. "Behind you!"

Juni spun around. He screamed! Then each Spy Kid slowly began to back away from the giant lizards. They didn't stop until they reached each other in the center of the clearing. Then they eyed the iguanas warily.

"Once again, the question is," Juni whispered, "fight or flight?"

Suddenly, Carmen gasped. She pointed at "her" iguana.

"Check out that spike on its head," she said.

Now it was Juni's turn to gasp. Glittering on the spike was a big, sparkly green ball emblazoned with the unmistakable logo: *Power Trip*.

"It's the treasure!" Carmen blurted. "For sure!"

"Which means we have to get it off that horn," Juni replied. "But how are we gonna do that?!"

Carmen tapped her temple with her finger and thought hard.

"Okay, iguanas are reptiles," she muttered. "Which means they're cold-blooded. And cold-blooded creatures don't move very fast, right?"

"Do we really want to test that theory?" Juni said in a quavering voice.

Before Carmen could answer, the kids heard a noise. It was a distant *clip-clop-clip-clop*.

"What's that?" Carmen said.

*CLIP-CLOP-CLIP-CLOP.*

"Whatever it is, it's getting closer," Juni said.

*Neiiiiiggghhh!*

"It's a horse," Carmen cried.

Correction. It was two horses. And on top of these horses were Rich and Allie Cheatham. They galloped into the meadow at full speed. Rich was heading straight for the iguana with the treasure ball. Without missing a hoofbeat, he leaned out of his saddle, plucked the ball off the iguana's horn, and continued riding. The iguana barely noticed. At the far end of the meadow, Rich trotted over to his daughter and handed her the treasure.

"Way to go, Daddy!" she cried.

"Way to go, indeed!" said a voice at the edge of the clearing.

Carmen and Juni spun around. Of course, it was Jack Crakst. He had just appeared at the scene with cameramen in tow. They'd captured the Cheathams' triumph—again!

"Wait a minute," Carmen said to the gloating dad and daughter. "This isn't over. Remember the poem: *'Is the find precious? No, it's not,* until *it's in a special slot.'*"

Jack glanced shiftily at the TV camera. Then he nodded.

"She's right, you guys," he called out. "Play on."

"Fine!" Allie said snottily. She and her dad spurred their horses and galloped out of the field.

"We have to catch up with them and get that treasure out of their slimy hands," Carmen whispered to her brother.

"How?" Juni said. "I don't see any more horses around here, do you?"

Carmen eyed one of the blue iguanas with a thoughtful expression.

"No . . ." Juni groaned.

"Yes," Carmen said firmly. Then, without hesitation, she began running toward one of the giant lizards. She vaulted herself onto its scaly back and grabbed one of its horns.

"Yah!" she cried.

The giant iguana looked over its shoulder at Carmen. It blinked its buggy, green eyes at her lazily.

"Yah, yah!" Carmen cried desperately. She tapped the lizard's belly with her heels. Meanwhile, Juni gingerly climbed onto the other iguana. It sat there just as impassively as Carmen's.

"Giddyup?" Juni pleaded. "Hi, ho, uh, giant lizard?"

"Please?" Carmen begged.

Juni groaned in frustration. The *clip-clop-clip-clops* of the Cheathams' horses were barely audible now.

"C'mon, guys," he said to the iguanas. "What do we have to do to get you to chase down those horses? Promise to take you home and make you our pets or wha-*AHHHHH*—!"

Apparently, Juni had said the magic word. Because his iguana suddenly darted forward with the swiftness of a tiny salamander! Carmen's lizard was right behind them. The kids grabbed onto the iguanas' horns for dear life as the creatures plunged into the forest. Satisfyingly, they left nosy Jack Crakst and the TV cameras in the dust.

And even more satisfyingly, the *clip-clops* were getting louder.

"I guess my cold-blood-makes-for-a-poky-lizard theory was wrong!" Carmen cried with a grin.

"Hey, I see them!" Juni yelled with a grin of his own. He pointed up ahead. The Cheathams were careening through the trees. They were headed for the beach.

"After them!" Juni yelled at his iguana. The lizards scurried even faster. In an instant, they'd caught up to the horses.

And just in time!

"Juni, look!" Carmen yelled, pointing down the beach. A box was perched on a tall pole. There was a target painted on the box. And in the center of that target was a hole. Clearly, the treasure ball was meant to be lobbed through the hole.

"We can't let them get close to it!" Juni huffed. He spurred his iguana on and darted ahead. Soon, he and Allie were neck and neck, dashing across the sand.

"Be careful," Carmen called out to her brother.

"Don't worry," Juni replied from his leaping lizard. "I'm not getting anywhere near those hooves."

Allie turned to smirk down at Juni from her horse. As she galloped along, she called out, "Well, then, I guess I'll have an unobstructed shot at the target. Thanks for helping us win—again!"

"Are you sure you can throw it high enough?" Juni asked Allie, "with those skinny arms of yours?"

"Skinny?" Allie sniffed, glancing down at her biceps. "My arms are perfectly fine. Shapely, even."

"Oh-kay," Juni said in a patronizing voice. "Sure. Olive Oyl had shapely arms, too!"

"Listen, kid . . ." Allie began, shaking her head at Juni in annoyance.

"Oh, and you might want to run a comb through that hair," Juni added. He pointed to a couple of cameramen who'd just emerged from the jungle to capture the action. "You're on camera, you know!"

"What?" Allie cried in alarm. "My hair? What's wrong with my hair?"

Reflexively, her hand flew to her head. Unfortunately for her, it was the hand clutching the treasure ball! The glittery orb flew out of her fingers and landed on the beach with a plop.

"Girls are *obsessed* with their hair," Juni said to himself with a happy chuckle. "Works every time!"

Meanwhile, Carmen and her iguana made a dash for the ball. She scooped it neatly off the sand and stashed it under her arm. Then she began galloping toward the target.

But winning the challenge wasn't going to be *that* simple. Rich Cheatham was waiting for her! He had something under his arm, too—a polo mallet! And he knew how to use it. He galloped straight toward Carmen and swung the long, skinny mallet through the air. Carmen flinched. He was trying to hit her!

Correction—he was trying to hit the ball. And he did! With expert precision, he tapped the ball out from under Carmen's arm, leaving her without a scratch! The ball landed on the beach again. Rich chased after it and gave it a whack with his mallet, sending it sailing down the beach. Galloping after it again, he gave the ball another whack. He was nearing the target. He was going to shoot the ball into the hole with his mallet! Allie, having smoothed down her hair, was now cantering in her father's wake, cheering him on.

Carmen looked down at her empty hands. Then

she looked around the beach, desperate for a solution. All she saw were palm trees. And sand crabs. And *more* palm trees . . . hey . . .

"Juni!" Carmen yelled suddenly. "Grab me one of the biggest palm leaves you can find and meet me at the target."

"Why?"

But Carmen didn't have time to explain. Without another word, she raced off after evil Rich Cheatham. He was now only a few hundred feet from the target!

"Hurry, Juni," Carmen screamed over her shoulder.

Only a few seconds later, Juni and his lizard appeared next to her with a giant, fluttery palm leaf. It was at least six feet long.

With a grateful grin, Carmen grabbed the leaf and sprinted toward the target. Out of the corner of her eye, she saw Rich's polo mallet rear back. He was taking his shot!

*Thwack!*

Rich had hit the ball hard. The glittery orb was sailing through the air. But Carmen was still ten feet away from the target!

She gritted her teeth with determination. She watched the ball make a graceful arc through the air. She did a quick mental tabulation. Then she stood up on her iguana's back—and jumped!

Carmen sailed through the air with her palm leaf outstretched. She reached so hard, she went completely horizontal.

And it worked! Just before the treasure ball slipped into the target, it was intercepted by the very tip of Carmen's palm leaf. It bounced off the leaf and hit the beach.

"Yesssssss-OOOOF!" Carmen grunted as she hit the sand herself.

Now it was Allie who dismounted her steed. She began running for the treasure ball at full speed. Carmen struggled to her feet.

"Have . . . to . . . get to the ball . . . first," she huffed as she ran. She and Allie were coming at the treasure ball from opposite sides. They were both about a hundred feet away from it. But Carmen was weakened by her tumble. Was she going to lose the treasure again?!

The answer came in a flash of blue scales and a slithery tail. Juni and his iguana suddenly shot between the two running teenagers!

"Excuse me, ladies," he said as he scooped the ball off the beach. He steered his lizard toward the target. Rich Cheatham chased after him.

Juni sped up.

And so did Rich. He was closing in on the Spy Kid! But not fast enough! Juni was almost at the target. He would have only one shot. And he had to take it . . . *now*!

Juni hurled the treasure ball.

All four competitors held their breath as they watched it arc through the air. The ball glinted in the sun. It seemed to swerve to the right. And then the left. Finally—it hit its mark, slipping neatly through the hole and disappearing inside the box!

"Whoo-hoo!" Juni cried as his excited iguana continued to race madly down the beach. "Whooo—uh, whoa! Whoa, boy! *Whooooaaaa!*"

But Juni's iguana was apparently going so fast it *couldn't* whoa. In fact, the lizard and his passenger crashed right through a bank of elephant ear plants and disappeared!

Carmen was left alone on the beach with Rich and Allie, who were both red-faced and seething. She grinned at them in triumph.

"I think that's my cue to head on to the second leg of the challenge," she announced. "Smell ya later, Cheathams. And I do mean 'smell'!" she couldn't help adding.

Then Carmen smirkily waved good-bye to the

TV cameras and dashed after her brother. She plunged into the foliage after him. She spotted the tail of Juni's iguana in the trees up ahead and darted forward to meet him.

"I gotta hand it to you," she said as she approached Juni. "That was the sweetest save I've ever seen. You rock, Juni. . . . Juni?"

Carmen caught up to Juni's lizard. But the creature was riderless! It gazed at Carmen with a bored expression in its buggy eyes. Then it ate a dragonfly.

"Juni?" Carmen called, peering into the jungle. "Where'd you go?"

She was answered only by eerie silence.

Her brother had disappeared!

# CHAPTER 12

***S****ssssssssssss!*

Juni yelped as he felt himself being lowered into a body of water—a very *hot* body of water. Whether it was a big bathtub or some sort of volcanic spring, he didn't know, because he was blindfolded.

All Juni *did* know was that the instant he and his iguana had broken through the brush, someone had grabbed him from behind! That someone had tied a *Power Trip* bandanna over his eyes, bound his hands together, and led him through the jungle. And that's how Juni had ended up here, sitting in this bubbling, steaming water.

"Who are you?" Juni called out. "Show yourself, you coward."

"If you say so," a very familiar voice said. Juni felt a hand untie his blindfold. Then he found himself blinking up at Jack Crakst!

"Jack!" Juni cried. "What's the deal?"

Jack merely shrugged and flashed a smile.

"Um," Juni said hesitantly. "Listen, Jack. If this is some sort of 'spa treatment' to reward me for winning the challenge, well, I've gotta tell you, it's not so pleasant. So, I think I'll get out now."

Juni started to pull himself to his feet. With his hands bound, it was a struggle. As he flailed, the water began to hiss louder. Little bubbles rose to the surface. Juni felt the temperature get even hotter! He winced in pain.

"Yeah, I wouldn't do that if I were you," Jack said lightly. "You see, Johnny, you are sitting in the middle of an A.B.-level hot spring."

"A.B.?" Juni questioned with a scowl.

"Almost boiling," Jack explained. "The water is just one degree below boiling temperature. The slightest movement could stir it up just enough to bring it to a nice rolling simmer. Which would turn you into a nice, little kiddie meal. And, oooh, that would sure smart, wouldn't it, Johnny?"

"It's Ju—Oh, never mind," Juni said irritably. He stopped struggling and held his limbs as still as he possibly could. The bubbles disappeared and the water cooled a tiny bit. He sighed in relief. Then he turned his head to glare at Jack.

"I suppose the Cheathams paid you to kidnap me?" Juni accused, his eyes focusing in on the host.

Jack examined his manicured fingernails as he sniffed, "Please. I'm a highly paid TV personality. I don't need their money."

"Well, then," Juni sputtered, "why—?"

"Juni! I hear you! Where are *yooooouuuu*?"

That was Carmen! Juni started, causing a painful flurry of bubbles to rise in the almost-boiling spring. But he didn't care. Carmen was nearby! She'd be here soon. She would kick Jack Crakst's butt and figure out how to get Juni out of this soup pot!

Juni turned to flash a gloating smile at Jack, but he found himself blinking at the air. Jack had flown the coop! And only seconds before Carmen poked her head through the trees.

"What are you doing?" she exclaimed. "Mom can never get you to take a bath at home, and now you decide to scrub up smack-dab in the middle of our challenge?"

Juni sighed and rolled his eyes. He was *so* misunderstood. He patiently explained to Carmen everything that had just happened.

"Jack did this?" Carmen cried when Juni had finished his tale. "We've got to find him!"

"*We* aren't doing anything," Juni said, "until I get myself out of this almost boiling cesspool. We need to cool this water off!"

"If only we had our gadgets," Carmen lamented. "My Sno-Glow could turn this pond into a rink in no time. Let's see . . . cold . . . cold . . ."

Suddenly, Carmen gasped.

"Of course," she said snapping her fingers. She cupped her hands around her mouth and called, "Bluebell! Oh, *Bluuue*-bell. Here, girl!"

The kids heard a rustling in the jungle. Then Carmen's giant blue iguana peeked shyly into the clearing.

"Bluebell?" Juni snorted. "You named your iguana?"

"Hey, we promised to take them home as pets," Carmen said. "And that means naming them. I thought we could call yours Babe the Big Blue Iguana."

"Um, that sounds great, but could we get back to the matter at hand?" Juni said, glancing down at the steaming-hot spring.

"Oh, right," Carmen said, stroking Bluebell's spiny head. "Let's see if this works. Bluebell, turn around, please."

Obligingly, the lumbering lizard turned away from the pond. Carmen dipped the iguana's giant tail into the spring.

*Sssssssssssss!*

The water emitted a big puff of steam. Then it stopped almost bubbling. In a few seconds, Juni was sure the water had cooled a few degrees. Gingerly, he kicked one leg. No boil! The cold-blooded reptile had cooled things off!

"Yahoo!" Juni cried, jumping to his feet and scrambling out of the spring. He patted Bluebell's scaly back in thanks. Then he turned to his sister. "Let's go do some spying on our 'gracious host,' Jack Crakst!"

As the kids sneaked through the jungle, Carmen called their parents on her spy watch's walkie-talkie and told them the situation. Mom and Dad promised to rustle them up a tasty dinner while they spied.

"Get back to us as soon as you have your intel," Dad told them. "And children—be careful! If Jack Crakst is helping the Cheathams cheat, then we have no allies on this island."

"Roger," Carmen said. "Over and out."

The kids continued to slink through the jungle. Their sandals squelched in the swampy mud of the trail. Condensation from overhead leaves dripped onto their heads. It was positively eerie. *And* gross.

"I wonder how we'll find Jack," Juni whispered. "This isn't exactly a tiny island."

Carmen bit her lip. Juni had a point. Jack could be anywhere. Carmen scanned the jungle for clues. She saw nothing but a howler monkey scampering in a tree, the occasional butterfly, and another one of those rope bridges cutting through the treetops.

"Hey, wait a minute. . . ." Carmen suddenly exclaimed. She grabbed Juni and said, "Have you noticed that Jack's shoes are always spotless?"

"I guess," Juni said with a shrug.

"Well, that'd be impossible if he got around the island on foot," Carmen pointed out. "Look at your feet. They're filthy."

"Hey, yours aren't so clean, either," Juni retorted. "*And* they're stinky."

"My *point* is," Carmen said, rolling her eyes, "that clearly Jack uses those rope bridges to get around. In fact, I bet *he* told the Cheathams all about that bridge they used to win the first challenge!"

"Of course!" Juni said. "So . . . now what?"

"Now we follow the bridge!" Carmen said. "I bet it leads us right to Jack!" she said, knowingly.

They crept along beneath the bridge so they wouldn't attract any attention. The bridge swooped over streams and swagged over quicksand pits. It twisted and turned and loop-de-looped around the ancient native temple. But finally, it ended at a sumptuous campsite containing several shelters constructed of wood and canvas tarps. There was an outdoor kitchen where a crew member was frying up fragrant plantains. And from one little hut, the Spy Kids could hear the unmistakable voice of Jack Crakst.

Glancing around to make sure the coast was clear, the kids scurried over to the hut and crouched beneath one of its windows. Then, with the stealth that only highly trained spies can muster, they peeked inside. They saw two beauty shop–style chairs. Sitting in one of them was Margarita. A crew member was blow-drying her hair with the help of an electric generator.

"Rrrrrremember," Margarita admonished the hairdresser, "it must look perfectly natural." Then she picked up a pale pink lipstick and applied a glossy shine to her lips.

"She's totally ignoring the 'no cosmetics' clause in the fine print," Carmen whispered to Juni. "Mom's gonna be mad!"

Juni rolled his eyes and pointed to the other chair. There was Jack! He was speaking into a cell phone while another crew member painted white goop on sections of his hair and wrapped them in tinfoil.

"Queen bee?" Jack was saying. "This is drone number five. All is sweet here."

Jack paused to listen and take a slurp of a frosty fruit smoothie.

"Don't you worry," Jack said smugly. "Let's just say that little Johnny Cortez has found himself in a bit of hot water. Nothing can save him—certainly not his meddling sister. Heh, heh."

"It's Juni!" Juni whispered to his sister indignantly. She slapped a hand over his mouth and motioned toward the woods. The kids crept away as silently as they had come.

"Oh, man," Juni complained when they'd hiked out of earshot. "How hard is it to remember one two-syllable name? Ju-ni!"

"I'm more concerned about the name of the person Jack was calling," Carmen said with a frown. "Let's get back to Mom and Dad and fill them in. I think our mission just got a lot bigger!"

# CHAPTER 13

**W**hen Carmen and Juni arrived back at their campsite, Juni sniffed the air. He'd hoped to find the aroma of fish grilling or a coconut cake baking. But all he smelled was salt water and warm island breezes.

"No dinner?" Juni whined. "But I'm s*tarrrrrv-ing*."

"Shhh," Carmen said as they approached their parents. Mom and Dad were sitting on the beach, staring into Dad's spy watch. "It looks like they're doing some serious spying."

The kids stole up behind their parents and peeked over their shoulders. On the screen of Dad's spy watch was the tiny face of their boss, Devlin! Juni began to wave in greeting, but Devlin was displaying no trace of his usual charm. His mischievous eyes had darkened, and his rakish grin had turned grim.

"Well, Cortezes," he harrumphed, "so I guess

your mission was *not* accomplished. That's a first for you, but . . . don't worry. We'll just find another way . . . somehow . . . to foil the Cheathams."

"What?!" all four spies blurted.

"With all due respect, Mr. Devlin," Carmen said, "what are you talking about?"

Devlin held up a copy of *Novelty*, the Hollywood trade magazine. A headline on the front page read CHEATHAMS ARE JUST POINTS AWAY FROM WINNING *POWER TRIP*.

"But the game isn't even over yet," Juni complained. "And just a couple of hours ago, Carmen and I won a challenge. How did that story happen?"

"Somebody leaked it to the reporter," Devlin said with a furrowed brow. He read an excerpt from the article to the spies:

"'We at *Novelty* spoke to MYPQ network president Honey Combs about the Cheathams' heavy lead. "Of course, we can't divulge *Power Trip*'s winner until the show airs this spring," Combs responded. "And, of course, I have *no* comment on the fact that Keenan O'Ryan has booked the Cheatham family on his talk show just one week from tonight, eleven P.M., Eastern Standard Time, ten P.M., Central."'"

"That will be Allie's opportunity to unleash the Brain Beater on the unsuspecting TV viewers of the world." Carmen gasped. "We can't let that happen."

"How are we going to stop it?" Juni said glumly. "The Cheathams have even got the network president duped. Do you know how powerful a network president is? She's like Queen of the entertainment world!"

"Queen . . ." Carmen said with a frown. Then she gasped. "That's it! She's Queen Bee!"

"Huh?" said Devlin and Carmen's family in unison.

"With his cell phone, Jack Crakst was reporting to someone named Queen Bee," Carmen cried. "Queen Bee. Honey Combs! Get it?"

"And you know what else," Dad realized suddenly. "We're on Abeja Island. And you know what *abeja* means, don't you, children?"

"Bee!" Carmen and Juni gasped together.

"I never made the connection," Mom groaned. She slapped her sandy forehead with her palm.

"So, now we know," Juni said darkly. "The Cheathams are just pawns of a force even more powerful and evil than they are—fame! They don't have to use the Brain Beater to get all the attention. Honey Combs can give them that. And in return, *she'll* make them use the Brain Beater for her *own* gain!"

"The possibilities are staggering," Dad said.

"These villains could manipulate audiences into watching nothing but MYPQ," Carmen said, with wide eyes. "The rest of the entertainment industry would go bankrupt."

"They could force advertisers to pay extraordinary sums to show commercials on their network," Mom pointed out.

"They could make TV stars work for peanuts!" Juni added.

"Once Honey Combs has conquered the world of TV," Dad said, "domination of the *real* world is just a step away!"

Carmen sat down in the sand despondently.

"And her *first* step is making sure the Cheathams win *Power Trip*," she said. "We never had a chance. This game was rigged from the start."

"So . . ." Mom said, "our mission changes."

"Yes," Dad agreed. "But who's our new enemy? The Cheathams or Honey Combs?"

All the spies fell silent as they pondered their new predicament.

"One thing's for sure," Juni thought out loud. "If we're going to fight Hollywood, we have to stoop to their level. Hit 'em where it hurts."

"Okay, so what do TV types value most?" Carmen mused, rubbing her hair absently.

"That's easy," Juni said. "Their image."

Suddenly, Juni's sunburned, sand-scuffed, chapped-lipped face broke out into a huge smile.

"That's it!" he declared. "We're going to conquer Honey Combs and her evil followers with the worst weapon Hollywood has to offer."

"An excruciatingly long awards show?" Mom asked in confusion.

"Worse," Juni replied with a grin. "Bad publicity!"

Ten minutes later, Juni had filled his family in on his plan of attack. They looked at one another and nodded warily.

"In order for this plan to work," Dad said quietly, "our timing would have to be perfect."

"And luck would have to be on our side," Carmen added.

"All our spy skills would be put to the test," Mom said. "But I say, let's do it!"

Mom held out her hand. Dad slapped his hand on top of hers. Then Carmen and Juni joined in until all the Cortezes' palms had formed a stack of solidarity.

"We'll send the Cheathams and Honey Combs on a *Power Trip* to remember," Mom said.

"A trip right to the slammer!" Juni cheered. Then the spies broke apart and got to work.

JACK CRAKST: Hi, folks, Jack Crakst here. Let's check in on Camp Cortez. These mild-mannered computer consultants are no doubt frantic over the disappearance of their little boy, Johnny.

JUNI: Uh, it's Juni, Jack. And I'm not missing. I'm right behind you!

JACK: What?! But . . . but . . .

JUNI: Don't let the TV cameras see you looking so disappointed, Jack. By the way, your hair looks fabulous. Did you just get some highlights?

JACK: Don't be ridiculous. That's impossible. We're on a remote island. There isn't a blow-dryer for miles.

JUNI: Uh-huh. So, are you here to give us instructions for the next leg of the challenge? After all, I sunk the treasure ball in the target. Neat feat, huh?

JACK: Whatever. So . . . okay, fine! You want the next leg of the challenge? You've got it.

*Provided,* you can unravel this riddle. Good luck, Johnny. You'll need it!

While Carmen booted up the wireless modem in her spy watch to do some important computer hacking, Mom, Dad, and Juni regarded the slip of paper Jack had just given Juni.

"It's a haiku," Juni said. "Great. Now they're getting all artsy on us."

Mom read the poem aloud:

*It's a tangled web*
*To the crux of the matter.*
*To some, it's a snap.*

"'To some, it's a snap'?" Juni complained. "Yeah, to the Cheathams, who have plenty of inside information. This could mean anything at all!"

"I think it's some sort of existential quandary," Dad said, rubbing his chin thoughtfully.

"Or a philosophical dilemma," Mom said with a ponderous frown.

"Actually," Carmen said, looking up from her spy watch, "I think the tangled web refers to the rope bridge on the northwest end of the island. The 'crux of the matter' is a crossroads in two jungle trails near the bridge."

"And the snap?" Juni asked his sister incredulously.

"There happens to be a nest of snapping turtles right next to that crossroads," Carmen said triumphantly.

"Carmenita," Dad gasped. "I knew you were smart. I mean, your standardized test scores are excellent. But the way you figured out that riddle—I think you must be some sort of prophet!"

"No," Carmen said with a guilty shrug. "Just your average computer geek. I slapped a tracker on Jack Crakst's neck before he left. I've got a satellite read on him. And my spy watch says his location is at a trail crossroads at the end of the northwest rope bridge, next to a snapping-turtle nest."

"Oh," Dad said blankly. Then he smiled at his daughter. "Well, that was still some brilliant spying. Well done, sweetie!"

"Well, what are we waiting for? Let's get going!" Mom declared.

# CHAPTER 14

**W**hen the Cortezes arrived at the crossroads at the end of the rope bridge, they weren't surprised to find the Cheathams and Jack Crakst lolling near the trail. Allie was swinging lazily in a hammock, and Tate was teasing the snapping turtles by dangling tiny fish just out of their reach.

Everybody in the group—especially Jack Crakst—gaped in shock when the spies emerged from the trees.

"Don't look so surprised, Jack," Carmen said snidely. Then she gave her family a sly glance and added, "Of course, we were going to find you. After all, we're determined to win on *Power Trip.*"

"Ha!" Allie blurted. Then she shot one of the ubiquitous TV cameras a furtive look and covered her mouth.

"Well," Rich harrumphed, lurching out of the lounge chair he'd been lying in. "May the best family win. Let's get started, shall we, Crakst?"

"Of course, of course," Jack said, grinning at the camera. "This challenge is a three-parter. We'll need an adult to start things off."

"I'll volunteer, darling," Rich said to his wife.

Dad glowered at the arrogant Mr. Cheatham and stepped forward to challenge him.

"Gentlemen," Jack called. "Please, walk with me."

The two families, with dads in the lead, followed Jack down one of the trails until they arrived at the beach. A table was waiting for them. On that table were two unmarked green bottles and two crystal goblets. Jack held each bottle up and said, "We begin with wine tasting. You will each sample one of these bottles of wine and identify its variety, vineyard, and year. He whose guess is closest to the correct one will receive twenty points. The loser"—here Jack looked pointedly at Dad—"gets zilch."

"Gee, what a coincidence," Juni muttered to Mom and Carmen irritably. "Rich is a winemaker!"

"Don't you worry, sweetie," Mom whispered to him. "As you know, OSS spies exercise their taste buds as much as their muscles. Your dad's got a true nose for wine."

"We'll start with the challenger," Jack said, handing one of the bottles to Dad. "Go for it, Greg."

"That's Gregorio," Dad growled. He uncorked his bottle and poured some wine into the glass. He tilted the goblet this way and that, examining the wine's deep red color. He stuck his nose into the glass and took a whiff. Finally, he took a big swig of the wine, swished it around in his mouth, then spat it out in the sand.

"Ew!" Allie squealed.

"Hello! That's how wine tasting works," Carmen said in her dad's defense. "Swish and spit. Or maybe they don't teach you that at your fancy boarding school?"

"Just like they obviously don't give fashion tips at yours," Allie sniffed. She was sneering at Carmen's now tattered cargo pants and T-shirt.

"Girls," Margarita admonished. "Shhh. I think Grrrregorio is ready to rrrrrender his verdict."

"*Sí,*" Dad said defiantly. "This is a Merlot."

Juni could see Jack's jaw stiffen. Clearly, his dad was right!

"Le Vigneur de Papillon," Dad said, rattling off the vineyard's name with an impeccable French accent. Jack stifled a gasp, which must have meant Dad was right again.

"And the year?" Jack asked with a small tremor in his voice.

"The year is nineteen seventy . . ." Dad paused and wiped a trickle of sweat from his upper lip. He took one more swig of wine. He swished. He spat. And then he spoke.

"Two," he announced. "Nineteen seventy-two."

The Cortezes held their breath. Even the Cheathams forgot to look arrogant. They all gazed at Jack Crakst. For a moment, Jack looked stricken. But then a huge, falsely sympathetic smile broke out on his too-tanned face.

"Oh, I'm sorry," he cried. "But that is absolutely wrong, Greg. This is a Le Vigneur de Papillon Merlot, nineteen seventy-*three*. Too bad!"

Glowering, Dad stomped back over to his family. The spies watched warily as Rich stepped up to the table. He poured his wine, glanced at it casually, took a big swallow, smacked his lips, and said, "Ah, what a coincidence! This is a Château Margaux chardonnay. Château Margaux is named after my lovely wife, Margarita, of course."

"It's from his own vineyard?!" Juni sputtered. "That's *so* unfair!"

Rich glared at Juni and added, "And the date is 1989, the year my sweet daughter Allie was born."

Rich took another swallow of wine and smiled smugly at the spies.

"Right on the mark," Jack cried. "That means Rich will go first on the next part of our challenge. The big tee-off. Follow me, folks."

The competitors walked down the beach until they were standing opposite two yachts floating beyond the breakers. Well, *one* of the boats was a yacht. It was two hundred feet long and outfitted with a satellite dish, a full snack bar, and even a small pool. It was gleaming, beautiful, *and* big.

The other vessel was listing to the left, probably because its hull was full of rusty holes. Its paint was chipping off. Its deck was made of unpainted metal and was so fishy you could smell it from the beach! Hanging off the stern were a giant winch, cable, and hook. It was a lowly tugboat!

Carmen looked from one boat to the other and sighed.

"I've got a bad feeling about this," she whispered to her brother.

"The rules are simple," Jack announced. He reached into the pocket of his crisply pressed shirt and pulled out a golf ball and tee. He planted the ball in the sand.

"You simply hit the golf ball seaward," Jack said. "Whichever boat you hit will be your vehicle for the final *Power Trip* challenge—racing to a buoy five miles away. And since our points now add up to Cheathams, fifty-eight, and Cortezes, forty-seven . . ."

"Who knows how!" Carmen muttered.

". . . the Cortezes still have a chance to win!" Jack finished dramatically. "So, gentlemen, choose your weapons carefully. Ready, Rich?"

"R-ready . . . *hic*," Rich said. He staggered toward the ball and tee. Jack handed him a golf club. Rich grabbed it with an unsteady hand.

"Hey!" Juni whispered to his family. "I think Rich forgot to spit! He seems a bit unsteady. I don't care how many golf games he's played at his fancy country club—if he's tipsy, he could definitely make a mistake!"

"Let's hope!" Carmen said, casting the awful tugboat a dreadful glare.

Rich took a wobbly stance in front of the golf tee. He glanced casually out at the boats, then hacked at the ball with his club. The ball sailed into the air. It arced to the left. In fact, it was headed straight for the tugboat!

"Yes!" Carmen cried.

*Pzzzzzt. Pzzztpzzzt!*

"What's that buzzing sound?" Dad wondered.

An instant later, they could all *see* what it was. A

little jet of fire had begun shooting out of the golf ball. It had become a tiny rocket! And now it was flying away from the tugboat and heading toward the shiny white yacht.

"No!" Juni cried. But it was no use. The golf ball's rocket sputtered out just as it landed neatly on the yacht's spotless deck.

"A perfect shot by Rich Cheatham," Jack announced. "Now, on to *Power Trip*'s big finish! Whoever wins the race to the buoy wins the game!"

# CHAPTER 15

As soon as they'd "chosen" their boats, the families were led to small motorboats bobbing just off-shore. The Cortezes sighed deep sighs as a *Power Trip* crew member drove them to their decrepit tugboat. When they arrived at the rusty vessel, they climbed a fraying rope ladder to the deck. The crew member followed them, of course, with a TV camera.

The spies surveyed their boat.

"Well, the crow's nest is un-nestable," Juni observed, pointing to a large basket on top of a tall mast. There was a big hole in the basket's bottom, making it impossible for anyone to stand in it. "So, I guess we'll have to spot the buoy from the deck."

"Without any navigational equipment *and* a rusty steering wheel," Carmen noted as she peeked into the bridge.

Dad set his jaw and tied his *Power Trip* bandanna around his head. Then he turned to his family and tapped his temple.

"Like your Uncle Machete says, our best gadgets are these," he declared. "Our wits. So what if our boat is a little dilapidated—"

"Dad!" Carmen cut in. "It barely qualifies as a bathtub."

"True," Dad agreed with a shrug. "But *we* are international superspies. *And* we are Cortezes. And what can you always say about a Cortez, kids?"

"We're incredibly stubborn!" Carmen and Juni chorused.

"Right!" Dad said. "And *that's* what's going to get us through this race. Now, *you* boot up your spy watches' communications systems, and *I* will drive the boat."

Dad stalked determinedly onto the bridge and cranked the tugboat's engine. The boat emitted a wretched cough and a huge puff of smelly, black smoke. But, slowly, it began to chug out into the open ocean.

It only took a few seconds for the Cheathams' boat to glide past the Cortezes' tug. Margarita and Allie had already changed into bathing suits. They were lying in lounge chairs, sunning themselves. Tate was taking a dip in the yacht's pool. And Rich was at the wheel. He leaned through the window on the yacht's bridge and tweaked his hat—a ppy white seaman's cap, of course—at the spies. He looked the perfect part of captain.

"Ahoy, there!" he called cockily. "Remember to watch us next week on the *Keenan O'Ryan Show*!"

"Hello, Grrrregorio," Margarita added flirtily. "Aren't you the cunning captain!"

Mom glared across the water at Margarita, whose long black hair glinted in the sun as her yacht glided away. Mom fingered one of her scruffy dreadlocks. Her mouth tightened into a thin line. Finally, she stomped her foot.

"That does it!" she declared. "Gregorio, check the toolbox, please. Do you see a seven-eight donkey wrench in there?"

Dad rifled through a box of rusty tools.

"Yes, dear," he said, pulling out the heavy wrench. He handed it to Mom.

"Thank you!" Mom growled. Stashing the wrench under her arm, she whipped open a hatch door in the deck and jumped through it into the engine room. Soon, a series of loud screeches, clanks, and knocks began to echo from below deck.

"Whoa!" Juni said, peeking down into the engine room with wide eyes. "Mom's really mad. Good thing OSS basic training included shop classes!"

*Clank! SCRITCH! Whirrrrrrrrr!*

After thirty more seconds of Mom's furious tinkering, the boat emitted another cloud of smoke. But this time it wasn't black. And it wasn't stinky.

The engine stopped chugging and started humming.

The tugboat—which had been leaning heavily to the left—righted itself.

And Mom's voice rang out from the engine room. "Throttle it!" she ordered.

Dad yanked back the accelerator lever. The tugboat leaped forward! In fact, it moved so fast that both Carmen and Juni tumbled to the deck. But they didn't care. They were moving!

"Mom!" Carmen yelled. "You rock!"

"Look!" Juni called, pointing to the sea ahead of them. "We're already gaining on the Cheathams. They're so sure they're gonna trounce us, they're not even going at top speed!"

"Let's quiet down, then," Dad warned the excited kids. "We'll make a stealth takeover."

Carmen and Juni clamped their mouths closed and helped Mom climb out of the engine room. Then all four spies held their breath as their tugboat swiftly and silently began to overtake the Cheathams' yacht.

They got closer.

And closer.

"They've gotta hear us coming by now," Carmen whispered to Juni.

But the Cheathams were oblivious! It helped that Allie had cranked up some dance music and was bopping around the deck. And Tate was splashing loudly in the pool.

The distraction allowed the Cortezes to catch up with the Cheathams' boat, undetected. In fact, they sailed right past the yacht! That's when the Cheathams finally noticed them. Carmen and Juni giggled with satisfaction as the villains gaped in shock at the now speedy tugboat.

"Hello, Rrrrrrrich!" Mom called out flirtily. "Aren't you the sluggish shiphand!"

Rich was so stunned, it took him a full ten seconds to crank the yacht's engine up to full speed. By the time the Cheathams began racing after the tugboat, the spies had a healthy lead.

"We might actually win this thing fair and square!" Carmen marveled.

"Don't say that!" Juni cried. "Remember Regulation C-twenty-two, the Jinx Code? Never declare victory midmission."

No sooner had Carmen slapped her forehead in guilt than the tugboat began to lose speed!

Dad jiggled the accelerator. He hit the turbo-boost buttons. He even threw some ballast overboard. Then he threw up his hands in confusion. The tug's engine was still humming, but the boat was inexplicably creeping to a standstill.

"The Cheathams are approaching!" Mom cried. "We have to figure out what's going on!"

Juni frowned in thought. Then he got a suspicious look on his face and raced to the back of the boat. He peered over the railing and cried out, "Just as I thought!"

"What?" Carmen yelled, running to join her brother. She peeked over the railing.

"Ew!" she shrieked. "What are those?"

"Read the fine print," Juni taunted. "They're supersucking squid. Three big daddy ones, from the looks of them. They've attached themselves to our hull and they're sucking for all they're worth. They're dragging us back!"

Mom ran over for a look.

"Well," she proposed, "we could grab some wet suits and harpoons and jump overboard for a fight. . . ."

"But that would take precious minutes!" Carmen cried. She pointed at the swiftly approaching Cheatham yacht. "We need an Insta-Fix."

Suddenly, Juni grinned. Then he began to dig into the pockets of his frayed cargo pants.

"Insta-Fix in hand!" he announced.

"Rocks?" Carmen asked as Juni pulled out two handfuls of gray, oval things.

"Clams!" he announced. "To be more specific, these are clam bombs Tate and I made during our disastrous dinner party."

"Guess it was worth the humiliation, after all!" Carmen said with a triumphant fist pump. "Let's just hope these squid are in the mood for a little shellfish."

Juni tossed the clams overboard. Then the Spy Kids hung over the railing to see what would happen. Six buggy squid eyes followed the mollusks as they floated through the water. The squid seemed to pause for a moment, torn between sucking on the ship's rusty hull and snapping at the snacks.

Finally, their appetites won out! The squid unstuck themselves from the tugboat and made a grab for the clams. And it was at that precise moment that . . .

*Pow! Powpowpowpow!*

The clam bombs exploded gushily beneath the water! In response, the terrified squid spat out squirts of camouflaging ink. When the black ink clouds dissipated a moment later, the kids could see that the supersucking squid had fled.

"Yes!" Juni shouted. He turned and waved at Dad, who was watching anxiously from the bridge.

"Full speed ahead!" he yelled.

"Aye-aye!" Dad called. The tugboat gunned forward. And just in time! The Cheathams' yacht had caught up with them. The two boats were now racing neck and neck!

The yacht inched a few feet ahead.

Then the tug shot ahead and overtook the yacht.

Then the yacht was out front.

Then the tug!

It was anyone's race! And neither side could afford to lose. The tension on the Cortezes' tug was excruciating. The only thing that could break it was—

*Beeep! Beeep! Beeep!*

"That's my spy watch!" Juni exclaimed. "It's detecting satellite cell-phone activity on the Cheathams' yacht."

"Can you see the phone number?" Carmen asked.

"It's three-one-zero-five-five-five-six—"

"That's a Hollywood area code," Carmen

crowed. "The Cheathams are calling Honey Combs for instructions. Which means, it's time for me to get busy!"

With that, Carmen sat cross-legged on the deck and began typing wildly on her spy watch's tiny keyboard. After a few seconds of furious hacking, she looked up at her family and cried, "Done!"

"So you mean . . . ?" Juni asked breathlessly.

"Uh-huh!" Carmen said, glancing slyly at the nearby TV camera. "*Power Trip* is no longer on tape. We're all on live TV!"

"Live!" Juni said, with gleaming eyes. He waved at the camera.

"Live," Mom sighed, trying fruitlessly to smooth down her dreadlocks.

"Live!" Dad said eagerly. He typed something into his spy watch. Suddenly, a mechanical arm—capped by a wide, bowl-shaped device—popped out of the watch. It was a supersonic eavesdropping mechanism.

Dad made some adjustments to the eavesdropper, then pushed another button on the watch. Suddenly, the voice of Rich Cheatham rang out through the air. The Cortezes could hear everything that was taking place on the Cheathams' yacht. In fact, the entire TV-watching *world* could hear what was happening on the Cheathams' yacht.

"Ms. Combs," Rich was saying desperately. "The Cortezes—they're too good! I don't know if we can take them! How are we going to make it look like we really won if they reach the buoy first?"

"Ugh," said a slippery, soprano voice that clearly belonged to Honey Combs. "This is the treasure ball all over again. You really messed that one up! But this time, you will do *whatever* it takes to sabotage the Cortezes. Understood?!"

"Y-yes, Honey," Rich quavered.

"I'd be scared if I were you, too," Honey added. "I am *fiercely* devoted to my plan to take over the world by manipulating the country's TV-watching boobs. And *if* my plan fails, then so do you, Cheatham. No fame! No fortune! No riches!"

"B-but we had a deal!" Rich whined.

"Yes, but *I* know your little secret," Honey said threateningly. "You're no aristocrat at all. You've got no winery and no farm in the South of France. You've got a split-level house in New Jersey! You're just a boring accountant with stars in his eyes! And if you don't watch it, I'll leak *that* to *Novelty* magazine, too!"

"Oh, Honey?"

That was Carmen. She'd used her spy watch to

break into Rich and Honey's cell phone connection.

"What? Who is that?" Honey blustered.

"Carmen Cortez," Carmen said deliberately. "OSS!"

"OSS?" Honey Combs cried.

"OSS?!" all four Cheathams screeched.

"Yup," Carmen said smugly. She cocked her head. She could already hear the distant *flip-flip-flip* of an OSS helicopter, swooping in to take the Cheathams into custody. She knew, far away in Hollywood, other agents would be crashing into Honey Combs's office to arrest her as well.

"All four of us Cortezes are OSS," Carmen repeated for the criminals. "Which means, you're all under arrest. Oh, and guys?"

"What?" the Cheathams snapped.

"Smile," Carmen declared. "You're on candid camera!"

Juni slipped on his sunglasses and sighed happily as he lay back on his chaise lounge. An ocean breeze ruffled his curls. His belly was full of grilled lobster and coconut pie. He was almost completely content. But not *completely*.

So, Juni lifted his head ever so slightly and called out, "Jack?"

Instantly, Jack Crakst was at Juni's side. He was wearing a waiter's uniform and a sheepish expression.

"Yes, Juni?" Jack said breathlessly.

"Could I have another strawberry-mango smoothie, please," Juni said. "And, this time, go easy on the lemon. The last one was just a tiny bit tart."

"Oh, I'm so sorry about that, Juni," Jack said. "The perfect smoothie will be coming right up!"

Jack hurried off to the galley. That's right—Juni was luxuriating on a yacht. In fact, it was the sumptuous yacht formerly occupied by Team Cheatham. After the Cheathams and Honey Combs had been exposed to the world as diabolical criminals and arrested, Devlin had rewarded the Cortezes with a little downtime. They'd been spending the past several days lolling on the yacht, sipping smoothies, soaking up the sun, and recovering from their grueling *Power Trip*.

"*This* is the life," Carmen said, pulling herself out of the pool and flopping onto the warm, wooden deck to dry off.

"Indeed," Dad said. He and Mom were playing cards at a small table nearby. Mom's ginger-colored curls had unraveled from their dreadlocks and were shining in the sunshine. Dad had shaved off his scruff and burned his sweaty old bandanna.

"You know what I think the best thing about this vacation is?" Mom mused as she deftly won a round of gin rummy.

"Hmmm?" Carmen asked lazily.

"There's no TV!" Mom declared.

Every Cortez laughed and nodded in agreement. Even Juni! He'd decided family beat fame any day.